The Anatomy of Travel

The Anatomy of Travel: Selected Stories

Inquiries regarding the English-language copyright
should be addressed to:
The Lontar Foundation
Jl. Danau Laut Tawar No. 53
Jakarta 10210 Indonesia
(http: www.lontar.org)

Publication of this title in the Modern Library of Indonesia series
has been made possible by the generous assistance of The Ford Foundation.

Template design by DesignLab; layout and cover by Cyprianus Jaya Napiun
Cover illustration detail from *A Flood Tourists to Indonesia* by H. Widayat.
Image courtesy of the OHD Museum of Modern & Contemporaryu Indonesian Art.

ISBN 978-602-6978-91-2

MODERN LIBRARY OF INDONESIA

GERSON POYK

The Anatomy of Travel
Selected Stories

translated by
Gill Westaway

with an introduction by
Yohanes Sehandi

Jakarta, Indonesia

Contents

Introduction

One of the distinctive features of Indonesian literature has always been local color—that is, the smells, music, vegetation, landscapes, dwellings, speech, weather and other elements of a particular place that can evoke nostalgia in one who is far away from home. In a literary work an author records spiritual and social issues from a village community or from the society of the region where he has been working. According to the literary critic Jakob Sumardjo, this phenomenon is only right and proper, given that literature is the product of a particular society and is a reflection of that society. The obsessions of that society become the writer's own obsessions. In that sense, the study of a work of literature becomes a study of its societal context—its aspirations, its cultural levels, its tastes, its views on life, and so on.

Jakob Sumardjo calls a literary work which portrays the spiritual and social issues of the society of a particular region "Indonesian literature with regional color" or local color. In his book *Pengantar Novel Indonesia* (*An Introduction to the Indonesian Novel*) he examines Indonesian novels published between 1970 and 1980. One author who is particularly skilled at portraying local color in Indonesian literature is Gerson Poyk, who hails from the province of East Nusa Tenggara (NTT).

According to the writer and critic Mursal Esten, there has been a pronounced and colorful emergence of regional culture in Indonesian literature since the 1970s. Among the many examples he cites, he too points out work by Gerson Poyk, particularly his novel *Sang Guru* (*The Teacher*).

Mursal Esten divides Indonesian literary works into two groups, which he calls first and second track Indonesian literature. First track Indonesian literature is that which is generally recognized as national literature—modern Indonesian literature since Balai Pustaka, Pujangga Baru, Angkatan 45, Angkatan 66, and now including works which reinforce Indonesian national literature and lean towards an urban color and flavor. Second track Indonesian literature comprises works influenced by local cultures of the archipelago, expressed in the Indonesian language.

The very latest views on regional color spring from the Indonesian literary critic Maman S. Mahayana. In an article he wrote about the future of Indonesian literature, Mahayana puts forward an interesting thesis on possible developments in Indonesian literature going forward since the *reformasi*/reformation movement of the early twenty-first century. In his view, the social-political changes, which have occurred very swiftly and which have taken us in the direction of unstoppable globalization, will in all likelihood force the development of Indonesian literature to follow two directions in the future.

First, the trend towards globalization and leaps in the progress of information technology will give Indonesian writers greater access to events happening in other parts of the world. Second is the influence of social-political changes at the different levels of the Indonesian administration, especially in the process of political and governmental decentralization with the introduction of regional autonomy since 2001. Apart from the fact that regional autonomy has moved forward and governance is no longer centralized in Jakarta, the sociocultural life of many regions in the outlying areas of the fatherland will certainly become more grounded, will take root and will revert to the regional culture. It is more than likely that problems local to the region will become the central themes of literary works in the future. The local ethnic culture and social issues which occur in the regions will become fertile soil for Indonesian authors who live and write in the different regions.

This is already true of Gerson Poyk, most of whose writing is concerned with life in rural Indonesia, particularly the short stories compiled in this anthology, *The Anatomy of Travel*. But first let me give a brief introduction to this Indonesian man of letters.

Gerson Poyk was born on 16 June 1931 in Namodale, Rote Ndao regency, in the province of East Nusa Tenggara (NTT). He died at the age of 86 on 24 February 2017 in Depok, West Java, and was buried in Kupang, NTT. From 1955 until the year of his death, Gerson Poyk was a prolific writer. His literary work dealt with spiritual and social issues arising in the society of NTT, as well as those of other regional communities in which he lived and worked. He wrote novels and short stories but also poetry and plays, and worked as a journalist. Many readers of Indonesian literature have been able to connect very easily with his works depicting life in NTT. Gerson Poyk has often been called the storyteller of the East, meaning eastern Indonesia.

As an observer of Indonesian literature from NTT Province, I have been tracking since 2010 the history of Gerson Poyk's writing and the works of literature which he has produced. After publishing some poetry and short stories in the journal *Mimbar Indonesia*, Gerson Poyk published his first book in 1964, a novel entitled *Hari-Hari Pertama* (BPK Gunung Mulia, Jakarta, 1964, 1968). In 1975 he published three collections of short stories simultaneously with Penerbit Nusa Indah, Ende, that is, *Nostalgia Nusa Tenggara*; *Oleng-Kemoleng – Surat-Surat Cinta Aleksander Rajaguguk*; and *Matias Akankari*. By the end of his life in 2017, Gerson Poyk had published thirty titles, that is thirteen novels, fourteen collections of short stories, one collection of poetry, *Dari Rote ke Iowa* (2015); a book of journalistic writing *Keliling Indonesia: Dari Era Bung Karno Sampai SBY* (2010); and one book of philosophical reflections entitled *Teroris Tidak, Damai Ya* (2017).

Let's have a closer look at the short stories of Gerson Poyk which are brought together here in this anthology. We can see that in these stories, the distinctiveness of Gerson Poyk's writing is the way he portrays regional or rural color. This color is seen in the themes of his short stories, in the characteristics of the protagonists, the names of the characters, the settings where the stories take place, and the plots of his stories, which are simple and straightforward. He can also be mischievous. One can very much feel that these stories were inspired by life in village society, especially the society of NTT Province. Gerson's works are also influenced by his one-time profession as a journalist for *Sinar Harapan* (1963–69) when he covered a number of important events in various regions of Indonesia and overseas.

When I read this anthology, I was immediately reminded of the journalistic reports of Gerson Poyk which were brought together in *Keliling Indonesia: Dari Era Bung Karno Sampai SBY* (Around Indonesia: From the Era of Sukarno to SBY) which contains 55 articles. Naturally Gerson Poyk's journalism is not the same as his literary work. His journalistic work prioritizes facts in the life of a society and what actually happens, whereas a literary work takes an abstraction of the life of a society and converts it into another reality, which is formed by a creative narrative imposed upon the actual reality of the society. This may be better or more beautiful, or indeed uglier or worse, than the objective reporting of events, because the work of a journalist is factual truth while the work of a literary artist is truth born of conviction.

The nineteen short stories in this collection can be grouped into several different thematic issues. *First,* the theme related to the spiritual and social issues of rural society are recorded in the stories: The Water Buffalo Sellers, Woven Cloth, When the Jackfruit Tree Was Bearing Fruit, The Thatched House with a Stone Wall, The Pearl Family, A Family of Wanderers, When I Became A Papuan, and Sesandu. The stories which particularly portray the spiritual life of village society on the island of Rote where Gerson was born is recorded in the short stories: The Thatched House with a Stone Wall, The Pearl Family, A Family of Wanderers, and Sesandu. *Second*, the theme related to the difficulties experienced by those living in urban societies is recorded in the stories: The Anatomy of Travel, An Impoverished Village Far Away from Anywhere, Karawang-Bekasi, Sandalwood Fans, The Pond of Gold, The Absent-minded Lawyer, Reconciliation, and December Floods. *Third*, the theme related to intercourse with foreigners is reflected in the stories: Between Beirut and Bali, An Aria to Travel, and Sculpture.

Most of the stories are narrated in the first person. This choice of narrative style suggests that Gerson Poyk feels comfortable telling stories in this way, as if these were his own personal experiences. What emerges is the product of an imagination which takes as its starting point the reality of experience. For example, in the story The Water Buffalo Sellers, Gerson speaks in the person of a school child who, together with his big brother, is selling water buffaloes across Flores, from Manggarai to the slopes of Mount Inerie in Ngada. The impression that emerges is not of the difficulty of selling water buffalo over a number of weeks but rather the wealth and variety of experiences faced by this child. This short story has a strong element of personal reality in it, as Gerson spent time in Manggarai when he was small.

Gerson also captures the inner life of Anna, a wife who shows perseverance in waiting month after month for the return of her husband who has gone out to sea whale fishing in the open waters of Lembata, in NTT. As she waits for her husband to come home, she weaves cloth as her livelihood, according to the Lembata tradition. As she weaves, she is simultaneously weaving the life of her own family. Gerson Poyk also describes the inner life of a certain widower who lives alone in the story When the Jackfruit Tree was Bearing Fruit, and the story of an old man living a life of hardship with his paralyzed son in the story Pond of Gold.

I found it touching to read the four stories set in Gerson Poyk's birthplace, Rote, a small island in the far south of Indonesia. These stories are: The Thatched House with a Stone Wall, The Pearl Family, A Family of Wanderers, and Sesandu. Reading these stories transports us to this backward area, to the poor life of a village. Using the first person, he tells the story of his family when he was small and they lived in a thatched hut on the beach with a wall made of coral stone. The only place to sleep was on a platform, and their tables and chairs were large rocks. The thatched hut with the wall of coral stone was infused with the strong smell of fish. The story A Family of Wanderers recounts the successes of four brothers and sisters from a poor family. The eldest brother becomes a Catholic priest and is posted to the Philippines; the older sister becomes a businesswoman selling hand-woven cloth in Australia; the narrator becomes a mathematics lecturer in a higher education institution in Jakarta; and the younger sister becomes a broadcaster for Radio Netherland in Holland. At one point, all four siblings return to Rote for a holiday and visit the home they lived in when they were small, the thatched house with a wall made of coral stone.

A few of the stories have an urban setting. They do not portray a life of success, prosperity and city glamor, however, but rather the life of a poor community living in the city. Their lives are miserable, as they are enmeshed in various problems. A young girl is obliged to become a prostitute. Two siblings quarrel over the division of property that they have inherited, which is torn down in the tide of urbanization. A lawyer defends corrupt people to gain employment rather than sitting unemployed in the village.

Another social issue which is has not escaped the scrutiny of Gerson Poyk is related to social intercourse with foreigners, as reflected in the stories: Between Beirut and Bali, An Aria to Travel, and Sculpture. This theme is taken up by Gerson Poyk in the first person of a journalist who has covered war in various countries in Europe and the Middle East, becomes a visiting lecturer in the United States, and falls in love with a foreign young woman.

In this collection of short stories, now rendered in English, the reader truly travels and is able to taste and smell the colors of the author's world.

Yohanes Sehandi

Reference Materials

Gerson Poyk. *Keliling Indonesia: Dari Era Bung Karno Sampai SBY).* Jakarta: Libri, 2010.

Horison, Vol. VIII, No. 12, December 1973.

Horison, Vol. XI, No. 9, September 1976.

Jakob Sumardjo. *Masyarakat dan Sastra Indonesia..* Yogyakarta: Nur Cahaya, 1982.

Jakob Sumardjo. *Pengantar Novel Indonesia.* Jakarta: Karya Unipress, 1983.

Maman S. Mahayana. "Sastra Indonesia Menatap Masa Depan" in *"Pengarang Tidak Mati: Peranan dan Kiprah Pengarang Indonesia.* Bandung: Nuansa, 2012.

Mimbar Indonesia, No. 21, 21 May 1960.

Mimbar Indonesia, No. 38, 17 September 1955.

Mursal Esten. *Sastra Jalur Kedua, Sebuah Pengantar.* Padang: Angkasa Raya, 1988.

Sastra, Vol. I, No. 6, October 1961.

Sastrowardoyo, Subagio. *Bakat Alam dan Intelektualisme.* Jakarta: Balai Pustaka, 1983.

Yohanes Sehandi. *Mengenal Sastra dan Sastrawan NTT*. Yogyakarta: Universitas Sanata Dharma, 2012.

Yohanes Sehandi. "Perihal Pelopor Sastra NTT Gerson Poyk" in *Pos Kupang*, 6 December 2017.

Yohanes Sehandi. *Sastra Indonesia di NTT dalam Kritik dan Esai*. Yogyakarta: Ombak, 2017.

The Anatomy of Travel

I really didn't know the names of those villages which could faintly be seen beyond all the rice fields as you looked southwards.

Even though I recognized that as far as the eye could see to the south there were vast expanses of rice fields trembling in the cold night. Even though I knew that to the north there was a beach with white sand with the waves lapping at its long shore. Even though I knew that beyond the beach was a vast ocean. And yet I didn't know where I was right then. To my left and to my right there was a total sense of vastness.

Really I should have been celebrating the beauty of the night, the sea, and the rice fields, with the song of millions of insects, but I was unable to concentrate because I had a high fever and knew that it was getting higher and higher. My thin dried-up body was not in good health. Was I yearning for a night of celebration? I could not say I was.

All I could say was that the night had brought me here now with a group of men who had been in good health, maybe soldiers, who had been on the convoy truck earlier. The rain and the cold night wind had stimulated them. And because they were all fit and healthy, they sang the whole journey long, chattering and shrieking likes babies on their mother's lap.

Now all that was gone. I had been left behind all alone by that convoy.

The fever and shivering were getting worse. I was less and less conscious of what was going on around me and, apart from the raging fever, I was tormented by the awareness that I was losing consciousness. One or two vehicles drove past but not one of them was prepared to move my sick body from that remote place to the nearest village where there would be lots of people, that is, people who would see that I had a fever. I was just wasting time. Just wasting my energy which was almost exhausted anyway.

I slept with all my faculties only half functioning. My hearing, my sight, everything was only half functioning. If possible I would opt for some omen of certainty in the midst of so much uncertainty. In this situation the only certainty was that soon I would give up hope, my heart would stop beating, and I would surrender myself to whatever would come next.

If I was not mistaken, it was already past midnight. The sky was still completely dark. Faced with this situation, I lay down on the road. I lay there for a long time drifting in and out of consciousness, when from afar I heard the sound of someone coming nearer and nearer. A *becak* with two oil lamps was weaving along the road from left to right to avoid the largest of the potholes. I stood up to stop the *becak*. In fact I now found it very difficult to even stand up. The sickness was already making me feel too weak. My enemy the sickness was ready to overcome my sick body, but my body was not giving in. I was conscious again but in another place. I was in the *becak* and my head, which was hurting because I had fallen on the road, was now cradled in a woman's lap. Oh, I had been helped by a human being like me! Let us rejoice that the world is full of human beings.

The *becak* stopped. I was helped down by the woman and the *becak* driver. We were in a place beside the beach. Seeing all the canoes and the trawling nets hanging up, despite my high fever, I was able to conclude that I was in a fishing village, comprised of four or five huts with roofs and walls made of coconut fronds.

It was still dark. I was helped out of my wet clothes and given a blanket plus food and drink. Thankfully I could still eat. Then I was sent to sleep on a bamboo platform.

The world receded. The fever left my body. The hut made of coconut fronds disappeared. So did the woman. I was well again.

Suddenly my head separated from my body!

My head was twitching on the ground not far from my body, which was still on the sleeping platform. I could not believe that my head had come off. I looked very carefully. My heart sank when I saw with my own eyes that my head was becoming more and more like a skull. Oh, I did not have the strength to observe this miracle that had happened before my own eyes! But suddenly a stranger came in without asking permission and tried to grab my most valuable possession. He came in through the window with the sea breeze. His body was dirty and sopping wet. Without hesitating I got up and pushed him to the door.

"Don't you dare touch my dearest possession," I said.

"It's mine, it's mine, I've been wandering all around the world looking for it and now I've found it here!' said the man.

"It's mine!"

"It's mine!"

"Prove it's yours!" I said angrily.

"I'm not afraid!" he said.

"I'm even less afraid than you. The proof that this is mine is that it's here," I said.

"I'll give you historical proof!" he said. "And you, sir?" he asked.

"History is just about memories. Prove it with something that is present now, something that is part of life," I said, refuting the possibility of him providing complete proof.

This man's smile pierced my heart. "But life conceived of like that is too broad, as vast as the sea, as vast as the sky, as broad as the space and the time that I am in now. I just want to help you, sir, and to prove that through history, what you say is your most valuable possession is in fact something of mine that had gone missing."

"So you just want to grab it, huh?" I boomed.

"I see it lying on the floor. Your most treasure possession has been snatched off and thrown on the floor. So I want to pick it up. Apart from the fact that it belongs to me," said the man.

"You scoundrel!" I bellowed at him. "Get out, get out of here!" and I threw him out.

Suddenly I understood how to discourage this uninvited guest.

"So let's proceed in the following way. You, sir, are going to prove that it's yours by using history, while I'll use reason, technology, and systematic thinking to prove that it's mine!" I said, feeling extraordinarily pleased with myself for having thought of this idea. "Now we're going to go to a laboratory," I said.

We went together to one of the most modern laboratories. But the educated young lab assistants let us down. After thoroughly examining it for some time, they returned with a broad smile and declared that this skull belonged to someone of the Malay race. One of them said that it was not a prehistoric skull but rather from someone who had just died.

"But you gentlemen need to prove with certainty that this skull is mine, not his," I growled at the bald lab assistants, who were observing us both intently through the thick lenses of their glasses.

"But we can't, sir. It's impossible. Because you two gentlemen are both human beings. Now if one of you were a monkey and one a human being, then that would be different."

We went to court. But our efforts failed not only in the military court but also in the civil one, because there had never before been an occasion where a person with a head had sued a person without one. Hearing a case with the person *in absentia* was a common occurrence. But the judge, prosecutor, and witnesses took fright and ran away when they saw us come into the courtroom without heads, carrying just one skull between us.

So we returned to the hut.

"I also have a life history," I said to him. "The latest bit of it was how I was left behind by a convoy because I was sick. I met a woman who nursed me back to health. Look, you can see that my skull is healthy, it's white without any bacteria making it decay."

"Actually you, sir, are still sick. You still have a high fever. And you still have your head on your body. Your skull is still attached. Everything still hurts. That healthy skull you see in front of you is unrelated to your life, sir, or to the life of anyone like you, sir," he said sitting down near me. "My narrative is a healthy one. My skull disappeared while I was happily listening to a radio broadcast on RRI [Radio Republik Indonesia] from Jakarta. In front of me was a glass of white coffee, some biscuits, and a newspaper. Then my most treasured possession was cut off by my political opponent!"

"You're an absent-minded fool!" I said.

"I assure you that my memory is as sharp as my thoughts."

"You really don't care!"

"Yes, I do. I'm a very systematic person."

"I'm a dean. I'm a university lecturer. If you don't believe me, sir, give me a moment and I'll call some of my former students."

My unknown visitor paused for a moment.

All around us was silence. There was only the sound of the wind blowing through the gaps in the windows and the walls of the hut. Then suddenly two more people came in, a young man and a young woman. I didn't know either of them but they were audacious enough to come straight up to me. First of all the young man.

"The skeleton inside your body is my skeleton," he said.

I had no patience with such impertinence. I kicked him so hard that he was thrown against the wall. While I was preoccupied dealing with the young man I had just kicked, his young woman friend grabbed me by the chest. She opened up my chest and said in a hysterical voice, "So this is where you've been hiding my conscience. It's here! It's here!" and greedily pulled my conscience out from my chest, and then put it in hers. Hey!

I was confused and began to panic. Which part of me should I defend first? My head? My skeleton? My conscience? All these people that I did not even know were tearing me apart. My head had been carried off by that professor. My skeleton had already been detached from my body. My conscience had already left my body. And I was still crying uncontrollably when all these people disappeared into thin air.

"Hey! Hey! Bring back everything! Bring it back!" I shouted.

But the shouting was useless. I sprang to the door and chased them. At the door I crashed into the woman looking after me. I was flung down in front of the hut. When I came to, I was covered in mud and sand.

The woman woke me up and helped me inside. She rubbed the sand off my body and made me lie down again on the bamboo platform. She gave me something to eat and drink, but I was only able to drink something. My body was still feverish. I sprawled out on the platform with my eyes wide open, staring at the roof.

While I was lying down, I saw that nearby the woman was busying herself with her own affairs. Probably because my fever had gone down I was now able to notice things clearly. This woman was about fifty years old. Her skin was already quite wrinkled. But you could still see that she had once been very pretty with a bit of help from powder and lipstick.

"Son, you were delirious and crying a lot. Maybe because you had a very high fever," she said. "But, I'm sorry, son, I'm not able to look after you tonight. I need to go to town, as what is on this plate is the last food we have."

I immediately understood what she was trying to say. But I just kept quiet, for if I had had money of course I would have asked her to buy something to eat for dinner that night.

But precisely because I didn't have a penny to my name, I had hitched a ride with the military convoy truck.

The woman tucked me in well, took her bag, and left.

That night I could not get back to sleep. But luckily the fever started to go down. I got up to urinate on the beach. As I walked I looked carefully at each hut in turn. I was alarmed. I guessed I was all alone in this group of fishermen's huts. All on my own. All I could hear was the sound of the sea and the night breeze. I walked cautiously and with trepidation in my heart.

I went back to sleep and woke up early the next morning. There was no one around yet. The woman from the night before had probably given up on me, because it was nearly dawn. I was sad as I suspected that she was embarrassed in front of her guest as she had not been able to bring home anything to eat. Maybe last night she had already done what she could for me by bringing me to a sort of general hospital there on the beach. Or maybe something had happened to her.

I did not know the name of the village. I did not know the woman's name. I didn't know the name of the *becak* driver. I only knew that they had helped me, protected me, and taken care of me. Maybe they would not reappear that day, and I did not have the patience to wait around for them.

I got up from where I had been sleeping and wanted to put on my trousers and shirt. But they were not there. I only had on an old batik cloth and my underpants.

In that house all I could find were a butter tin used for cooking, a plate and tin cup for drinking out of, and a spoon. That was all.

This was not a village, rather just a fishermen's shelter, I concluded. I went out to the main road, which meandered into the distance with the rice fields on one side and the open sea on the other.

From afar I saw an oil tanker making its way towards me. I stopped it. There were already two people sitting beside the driver. There was no more room. But they let me climb aboard and stand between the driver's cabin and the tank.

The vehicle moved off. I held on tight with my body wrapped in the piece of batik cloth from before. I clung on like a snail, but at least I still had my head, my skeleton, and my conscience.

The Water Buffalo Sellers

Finally we reached the foot of Mount Inerie. Goodness, were we tired! After tying up our water buffalo, Rofinus and I lay down in a place where there was lots of dry grass and looked up into the clear night sky.

We were in a very dry area on Flores. If you look up at the peak of Mount Inerie, don't expect to see a thick forest with lush green trees like in the Ruteng mountain range in West Flores where we had come from, bringing our water buffalo to sell in this rural area around this dry old mountain.

"I really don't get why people in this area slaughter dozens of water buffalos when they have a big party," I said.

"Sometimes even hundreds of them," said my companion, proud to be able to comment on the traditions of his native homeland. "Probably in the old days this area was very fertile, seeing how close it is to the volcanic Mount Inerie."

Yes, he had been born in a small village at the foot of this mountain. He understood well how important it was for the people to have water buffalos for their celebrations.

After finishing elementary school, I had farmed the land for two years and looked after buffalos. When I was already quite grown up, I met Rofinus, a mature man who was illiterate and who took me on at the tender age of fourteen to show me the way and help trade the buffalos.

Then we fell silent. We slept well, being so tired, and woke up startled by a terrible commotion. Oh no! Once we got up, we realized it was just the sound of a ship's horn and anchors being put down. A KPM ship was in the process of docking in Aimere harbor, a small port near Mount Inerie from where they transported produce to Java.

"I'm hungry, Rofinus," I said.

"There's no water here," he said.

"We've got rice, cassava, corn, and *dendeng* [dried meat], right? Let's just cook it all over a fire and tomorrow we'll find water to drink." I said, looking around at my surroundings in the dark night.

The moon was illuminating everything—Mount Inerie, the sea, the coconut palms. In the distance we could faintly see the lights flickering on the KPM ship and hear the sounds of activity as it loaded and unloaded its cargo. Occasionally the sound of a motorboat could be heard amidst the flapping of the palm fronds in the night breeze. The area at the foot of this mountain looked as neat and tidy as someone's yard, as it had already been shaven bald by the dry season weather. On these grasslands grew Palmyra palms, challenging the very dryness with their straightness.

"Are there any fields being cultivated around here?" I asked.

"Of course there are, but I don't know if there are any field huts with anyone living in them," he said, standing up and looking around him. "Let me have a look over there in that valley!"

I stayed behind on my own looking after our buffalo. Soon Rofinus came back.

"There's a small hut beside that field," he said. "But there's no one there."

"And wasn't there any water?" I asked.

"I noticed that there was a spring in the middle of a dry river quite near the field. And, inside the hut, I saw a few clay pots. Let's go and check it out!" he said.

Before long, we were installed in the hut. We tied our buffalo to the fence and started organizing our dinner. Rofinus went to the spring he had found in the sand in the dry river bed while I cooked the dried meat. Then just as our rice was ready to eat, outside we heard the clip-clopping of a horse which stopped near our hut.

A man dismounted and peered in.

"Who are you?" he asked.

"We're here to sell our buffalo and are spending the night here in this hut so that we have somewhere to cook our dinner and sleep," explained Rofinus.

"Fine, but have you asked permission from my aunt?" asked the man.

"Oh, so your aunt's around, is she?" said Rofinus.

"Yes," he said.

"There was no one around when we arrived here," answered Rofinus.

"Maybe she's gone back to the village. Anyway it's fine. Just be careful with your fire. We don't want you to burn the hut down!"

"Thank you," said Rofinus.

"Thank you," he said.

Meanwhile the three men accompanying this man had dismounted from their horses, and came into the hut and sat down with us. Then one of them said to another one, "Teacher, best we just stay the night here."

When I heard this I felt relieved. It seemed that these were good people and I felt confident enough to ask him a question.

"Where have you just come from, Teacher?"

"We've been having a look at people digging drainage channels and at the river too," he said, adding a question of his own, "How many buffalos have you brought with you?"

"Just one," said Rofinus. "The buffalo belongs to my little brother here, and I look after it for him."

The teacher looked at me as if he did not believe him. "What have you brought with you to eat for dinner?" he asked.

"Not much, just this," said Rofinus, pointing to the rice in the cooking pot and the dried meat.

"We've got rice cakes with mung beans, sambal, and more dried meat," he said. "And don't worry, we've also got *moke* [fermented wine]. Let's relax together while we haggle over the price of your buffalo."

That night we had quite a party in that little hut. It was the first time I had drunk *moke*, which had a lot of alcohol in it and of course I got quite drunk. I felt as if I was floating, but I would not come down from the price I had set.

"Sorry, Teacher, I just can't bring down the price any more," I said.

"It's like this," began the teacher, "With a price like that you can buy a piece of weaving here. Then you can barter that piece of weaving for a goat on the way home, and then you can sell that goat for a good price in town! I'm helping you, son."

Although Rofinus was poking me in the bottom as a sign that I should not be tempted by this man's sales patter, I actually thought that what the teacher was saying made a lot of sense. I once had bought a goat and taken it to the town. It was easier to sell a goat than a water buffalo. Besides, the smell of buffalo sweat turned my stomach. Taking a water buffalo anywhere was really tiring, as you had to keep whipping it to make it move forward, whereas with a goat it just trots along the road as you herd it from behind. And if it did refuse to walk, between us Rofinus and I could just carry it.

But if a water buffalo refused to keep walking, it was impossible for us. That was how I saw things. Luckily we had been able to make it this far, following the road along the river which, as it was, had taken us three weeks. Because of all that, I agreed to his deal. Not because I was drunk. I was still able to weigh up the options.

"Good," said the teacher. "And tomorrow my children will go to the village to fetch goat, rice, salt and *moke* so we can have a celebration in this hut," he said.

"But what's the special occasion?" I asked.

"No special occasion. We just have a party alongside digging the drainage channels. We slaughter a buffalo and invite lots of people to eat with us, and then everyone gets busy picking up stones and getting palm tree trunks to divert the river to here and the rest dig drainage channels."

And there were lots more such stories, but I was getting more and more unsteady on my feet and drifted off, only to be woken by Rofinus shaking my head and whispering in my ear.

"We're losing out here. We can sell for three times the price they're offering. Get up, let's run away while it's still dark."

On hearing his words, I got up. They were all fast asleep and snoring, drunk on *moke*.

"No, we can't do that. I've already taken a decision," I told Rofinus.

"That's no decision," said Rofinus, shoving me hard.

"What is it, then?" I whispered.

"That's the drunken twaddle of someone who's had too much *moke*. You're still just a kid but you drink like that!" he grumbled. "That's just their tactics to make us sell our buffalo at a cheap price. They're very wily."

"I may be young but I'm a good buffalo trader," I said.

"Ah, listen to you! Get up!" Rofinus pulled on my arm.

I stood up. Carrying our bundle of belongings, we crept outside, being careful not to wake up those who were snoring drunkenly. We went straight to find the buffalo—but it had already been stolen!

"I suspected those people were up to no good," said Rofinus. "While they were drinking with us, their friends made off with our buffalo. Very clever indeed."

Rofinus took out his dagger, but I told him to put it away.

"The buffalo's gone, the buffalo's gone!" I shouted.

"Heey! Wake up, the buffalo's gone," shouted Rofinus.

The man who they called the teacher and his side-kick woke up.

"The buffalo's gone, the buffalo's gone!" I shouted again.

"We need to be up front about this, Teacher," said Rofinus. "This kid's still learning about how to sell. Have pity on him! Have pity on us!"

"Naturally you think it's us. That doesn't matter," said the one they called the teacher, looking Rofinus in the eye. "Naturally you don't believe that I'm actually a teacher supervising a project to build dikes."

"We're not talking about whether or not you're a teacher. We're talking about what's happened to our buffalo!" said Rofinus.

"But what am I supposed to do about it! Before I give you the money, you guys should make sure your buffalo is properly looked after. It's your fault!" he said.

I tugged at Rofinus's arm as they rode off on their horses leaving us behind.

"This is hopeless!" I said. "Never mind. We've still got enough money to get home."

"Ahh!" Rofinus grabbed his dagger and sliced into the earth. "Let's have a wash before we go and report this theft to the police," he said.

We went down to the dry river bed where in the middle there was a spring.

We walked with tired steps. My heart was heavy and my head dizzy. Never mind! I would just enjoy myself. But Rofinus was not conscious of what he was doing. He had already cut away swathes of vegetation with his sharp dagger as we walked down to the dry river. When we got there, we found it was already occupied by a water buffalo. Our very own water buffalo! It looked like the fence that we had tied it to last night had been rotten. Heavens!

Rofinus picked me up, twirling me round and round. We spun around and around like a top. Seeing us like that, our buffalo mooed. Mooed and mooed and mooed!

In the distance the ship's horn wailed, wishing us a pleasant stay.

An Impoverished Village Far Away from Anywhere

My husband has just got home from field work in a very poor area. Thank God he has returned safely, which means that the Lord has granted all the prayers I sent while he was far away from me, prayers that he is always free from danger. How I always must pray, knowing that he is a government agriculturalist who must go from village to village, rice field to rice field, from river to river, whether there are floods or not. All this is ripe with possibilities of a natural disaster. I am constantly afraid that he might slip over the side of a ravine, for example, or get swept away by a flood or get bitten by a snake. Ah, but let's not keep revisiting these dark thoughts that always haunt me. My husband has already come home safely. I feel I have come out on top of all those millions of pretty women scattered throughout those poor villages.

Yes, aside from natural disasters, human beings can also be dangerous for me. My husband is a man who—as he likes to boast to me every day—is prone to be attracted to pretty women, just as he was attracted to me when I was in the flower of my youth. Nevertheless I still believe that the pleasure of being drawn to pretty village women will not override the pleasure derived from the responsibility he feels towards his children. Yet I am still scared, especially if he goes into someone's house with that wound on his left shoulder.

My husband does not say much. When he came home with that wound, he just kept quiet and put his bag down along with some cabbages and fruit soon to be devoured by my children. Then he went off to the bathroom. I was reluctant to ask him about it straight away. I was sure that soon he would tell me all about what had happened to him.

While he washed off the dust of his journey—I mean to say, he bathed and changed his clothes—I set the table and served him the freshest food we had, eggs, and all kinds of vegetables which he had brought back from his journey.

After prayers we started eating. I still had not asked him about the wound on his left shoulder. We both ate in silence. I was very happy because his appetite was not affected at all. That showed me that his heart still belonged to me. The old saying that the way to a man's heart is through his stomach seems to be borne out in the relationships between men and women the world over.

Only when we were resting did my husband tell me calmly what had happened to his left shoulder.

"I nearly died," he said sighing deeply as he stretched out beside me. "All because of that *becak*," he added slowly.

I got up and took hold of his shoulder, impatient to know what had happened. "A *becak* driver attacked you?"

"No," he said. "I arrived at a district town on the beach which is always affected by flooding in the wet season and is dry and dusty in the dry season. The people really suffer as a consequence."

"They must be starving," I said, touching the wound on his shoulder.

"No, it's not as bad as that. The town's not far from the forest, so if there's nothing else to be done, they can go into the forest which is admittedly pretty harsh and fight with the wild animals to get a morsel of food to ward off imminent death."

As a woman familiar with fairy tales about the forest, when I heard this, I hoped that my husband had not become mentally ill. I did not really understand how such a sickness might manifest itself, but I guessed that it would probably cause hallucinations. But, no, it was not possible, it would not happen. My husband was still behaving normally. I was probably just over-sensitive about him being safe. Where on earth might such forests full of man-eating wild animals exist in an area that was close to Jakarta? After all, it was not as if my husband was travelling to districts or provinces that were a long way from Jakarta, was it? I kept quiet.

"This poor area must get good irrigation as quickly as possible. If not, the people will continue to get eaten by wild animals," said my husband.

He took a deep breath before continuing. "The floods and the droughts make it impossible for the people of this town to get a reasonable yield from their crops. And although the land there is fertile with first-class rice fields, it's all owned by rich people, who are like kings lording it over thousands of men hoeing the land and women planting and harvesting the rice, who are paid a pittance. If the workers are no longer needed, they creep off into the forest."

"But what do they do in the forest?" I asked, caressing my husband.

"They take on whatever work they can. They become *becak* drivers, robbers, prostitutes, whatever it takes to put food on the table."

I laughed at what my husband was telling me.

"Oh, my love, what you're calling a forest is actually Jakarta, isn't it? Don't be so pessimistic, my love! Jakarta's not a forest, it's a big city. Here there are skyscrapers with bright neon lights, music and dancing. Rows of shops selling imported goods, cars stacked up like sardines in a can. Banks replete with dollars and rupiah. A president and his ministers. Plenty of technocrats who are going to establish a modern industrial country. Artists who come and go: writers, painters, composers. Isn't that what our city's all about?"

My husband got up and said, "Please get me a glass of water." He sighed again. "I'm fine, even though my shoulder is wounded."

I got him a glass of cool water. I always kept the boiled tap water in a clay vessel which my husband bought in Banjarmasin.

"Sure, a city's a city and a forest's a forest from a visual point of view. From a sensory point of view—I mean if we comprehend it in terms of the five senses, instinct and reason—yes, Jakarta is a city. But if we look at Jakarta and forests from a total life perspective, then Jakarta is a desolate place, just like the forests of Kalimantan— where the jug we're drinking our water out of came from." Then my husband took a deep breath, puffing out his strong broad chest, one of the things I found attractive about him.

"What exactly do you mean by desolate?"

"Desolate in terms of the social regulations, which follow the religious teachings on love that stem from God Almighty who always declares His love for us."

I had often heard my husband talk like this. He was someone who liked helping other people. Oh, if I think about it, actually we could have been rich long ago. We could have owned dozens of hectares of rice fields through his work at the Ministry of Agriculture. But my husband's philosophy of life is different from other people's. From his point of view, we had enough money to meet our basic needs. As for luxuries, he stubbornly persisted in changing my way of looking at things, saying all that was primitive, comparable for example to eating human flesh. Just imagine, once we had five hectares of first-class rice fields in the interior. Then when bands of armed thugs started making trouble, nobody took care of the land. I needed to say that before I continue with the story of my husband.

In the period that my rice field was looked after by someone else, we got a fifth of the yield and the rest was for the worker. Imagine how strange. When that worker was robbed and killed, we sold the land, as my husband was transferred to the city. With the money we got for the land, we bought two cars of our own. But my husband didn't like the way Jakarta folk were crazy about owning their own cars. The streets of Jakarta were chock-a-block with cars. Jakarta had become a forest full of barbarous cars.

So we exchanged our cars for a public bus, serving the public, not to get too big for our boots. But surely Jakarta was full anyway of people living there who had cars. I didn't want to become an animal, or feed on the flesh of others. But that was what my husband complained about.

So that's how it was. All the wealth that we had accumulated over the years became public property. But in the end I understood, although to begin with we used to quarrel over this to the extent that it almost ended in divorce.

Akh, I forgot! Now I needed to be thinking about my husband's shoulder.

"So what happened then?" I asked.

"My dear wife," said my husband. "I reached that district town at night, just after it started raining. After dinner, I took a *becak* to get to where I needed to go, a village some eleven kilometers from the town. I asked whether it was too muddy, but the *becak* driver said it wasn't. I got into the *becak* and we made very slow progress. We talked about everyday things. The *becak* driver told me that he used to drive a *becak* in Tanjung Priok. One night his wife ran away with another man. So he brought his children back to his village in the country, not far from this poor district town. He didn't have any land. After meeting up with a guy who owned a *becak* business, life for himself and his children had taken a turn for the better."

"But darling, I want to hear about your shoulder, not about the *becak* driver." I couldn't help feeling impatient. My husband was always like that. Whenever he talked about himself, it always got tangled up with lots of stuff about other people's lives. I know his character. He always protects himself by lumping himself together with other people. But fair enough, as his wife of many years, it was understandable that I was impatient to hear about his shoulder injury. I was afraid he was suffering.

My husband continued, "We had reached a dark place when we got stuck in the mud, as the road which used to be hard had got chewed up while the government officials just got fat on their own power. The *becak* driver tried and tried to push, turning the *becak* to the left and to the right, peddling and peddling, getting down again to push, panting. I insisted I should get out and pay the original agreed fare, even though we were still far from my destination."

"So then you went on foot, darling?" I asked, caressing my husband.

"Yes, I walked. For several hours. I was tired and very sleepy. I tried sitting down to rest on a rock. But there were swarms of mosquitoes. So I went on walking slowly, and then I came upon a cart that was stopped by the side of the road. I got onto the cart, or maybe it was a truck, which was full of cement sacks, which was not a bad place to lie down on. But here too there were millions of mosquitoes that kept biting me, so I had to continue my journey scratching myself all the way."

Only then did I realize that my husband's body was covered in mosquito bites. Oh, I felt bad that I had only just paid attention to my husband's skin. What a negligent wife I had been, and to make up for that, I continued to caress my husband.

"I walked and walked, so tired and sleepy." My husband took a deep breath as if he were releasing the last of his fatigue. "I felt as if I was sleep-walking. I heard the sound of the cocks crowing at dawn in the villages I walked through. But everything—the rhythmic sounds of the insects and the frogs—just made me feel more and more sleepy. The road was very dark, as there were trees growing close together on both sides. My feet were groping around on the road and my shoes kept getting stuck in the mud. Suddenly my shoulder was struck by something sharp which made me fall down. Before I was fully conscious, I heard people fighting and the sound of a piece of wood being dropped..."

"Who were these people, what wood was this, darling?" I asked. "Oh, Lord! Then what happened? Who took care of you, darling?"

"I was taken to a sort of hut, then I slept until the next day. When I got up in the morning I found that I was in the middle of a remote village. All the men and women were already at work in the rice fields. At my side there was a woman asleep."

My heart began to beat faster and I frowned.

"Don't be jealous, darling. This woman was one of the most despicable creatures on this earth. She had leprosy. But luckily the farmer who had crashed into me was a good man and had not stolen my backpack. I slung it over my shoulder and went down to the river where I took out my soap and scrubbed my body with it probably as much as ten times."

I kissed my husband and prayed that in ten or fifteen years' time, the incubation period for leprosy, my husband or I would not be struck by such a calamity which could mean losing fingers or a nose.

Karawang – Bekasi

Chairil died very young. If he were still alive, I would treat Dudung and give him travel money to go home. Before they parted, Dudung would push Chairil to change the words of the poem which went: *we may be just scattered bones but they belong to you,* to become*: we may be just bits of scattered flesh but they don't belong to you….*

Maybe you still remember, one day we read in the newspaper that Jatiluhur Dam had burst. Because of such news, the newspaper where Dudung worked sent him to check it out. And one afternoon Dudung set out on his Javanese 1962 Czechoslovakian-made motorbike, which according to the office inventory was worth about as much as the panic to cook a corrupt official's baby porridge. Dudung "naar boven"—Upward-bound Dudung—was launched.

Dudung arrived there in the morning. But blow me down! That giant man-made lake was as tranquil as ever. There was just a rumor that at the far end there had been a landslide. A few people had been killed. Some fields had fallen down the steep mountain slope. So Dudung went off to the far end of the lake. After travelling for a few kilometers along the muddy main road to the west, his motorbike got stuck in the mud. That took some effort! He dragged it to another place which was even more muddy, but it was very difficult to turn the bike round. Dudung had no choice but to wait for the sun to dry out the mud. It was already about one o'clock. Dudung slowly made his way back as the rain continued to fall. In

this season there were bursts of sun and then more rain. But he had
to continue his journey.

Dudung stopped a few times to eat and drink and had a look
around as he talked to the little people. (Oh the arrogance of it!
If Dudung was such a big man why was he out here taking care
of this Jatiluhur business on a motorbike worth no more than the
panic over a corrupt official's baby porridge? And if Dudung was
so small, why was he handling Jatiluhur? In reality Dudung was a
balloon that was big when blown up and small when deflated. And
he was porridge. And this made him disgusted with himself. He
wouldn't admit that this was the case, because he wanted things to
be different.)

Day became night and he was still skimming over the fertile
northern plains of West Java. The cars with their headlights glaring
roared past him. The world appeared empty of humanity, with only
a sense of revulsion with life as a balloon filled with porridge.

All of a sudden he was hailed by two young girls dressed in
sarong and *kebaya,* like two baby chicks.

"Take us with you, sir!" said one of them.

"This is a motorbike, not a car," said Dudung.

"Come on, there's still room for two on the back," said the other
one.

So within no time at all Dudung's motorbike had grown
branches. If the motorbike was like a pair of glasses, now the
glasses had three branches. These absurd branches were bouncing
around from side to side as if they were dancing in the dark night
as they skimmed over the fertile plains of West Java. Through that
branched pair of glasses Dudung looked out at the world, searching
for humanity. But all he saw was the glare of headlights in front of
him whooshing by. This journey on his branched motorbike was
devoid of humanity.

But don't forget—behind Dudung sat two of God's creatures. Why the need to look any further than that for human beings?

"Where are you two going"? said Dudung.

"Don't know!" said one of them, giggling like a little hen.

"Ah!" said Dudung loud enough to be heard over the noise of the motorbike engine.

"You can throw us off on the side of the road or you can take us to Jakarta, whatever!" said the one sitting right at the back of the motorbike.

"Ah!" said Dudung again.

"Do you have parents?" Dudung asked.

"Yes, we do," said one of them.

"What does your father do?"

"He's a farm laborer."

"And your mother?"

"Don't have a clue. She just likes wandering around."

What a mess! Where on earth was Dudung going to take these two little creatures? When he saw them in the light of the headlights, these two were too young to be creatures of the night (they still giggled like small children). The night was too vast, like a vast ocean for them to swim in, but the strange thing was they were already swimming in the solitude.

"Sir, sir!" one of them shouted as the motorbike emerged from a small lake in the middle of the road.

"Stop, sir, my sandal's fallen into the water."

"What?" Dudung stopped the motorbike and looked behind him.

My goodness. No wonder the sandal had fallen off, given the way they were both sitting. They were both perched on the high seat with their feet hanging down swinging back and forth. The one in the middle was not actually wearing any sandals, but the one at the back was wearing one blue plastic sandal. (He could see the color blue in the light cast by the rear lamp of the motorbike).

So more work! Dudung turned his bike round so that it was facing the "artificial" lake in the middle of the national road.

Who would have supposed that Dudung would become a sort of film director, a cameraman, a lighting man, training the lamp onto the lake which measured approximately five by ten meters, while the two girls, with their sarongs pulled up to their thighs, groped around with their feet in the muddy water. If a car with glaring headlights whooshed by and splashed them with water, they just laughed. He wasted more or less an hour giving the two girls the chance to look for one cheap plastic sandal.

But in the end it was all for nothing. They both sat back down neatly behind him, with their legs hanging freely. The one who was not wearing sandals had a face like the flight stewardess called Isye whom Dudung had met on a flight to Bali. Why did Dudung suddenly think of the face of that stewardess? That wasn't difficult. On one flight when he was part of a group from the Ministry of Agriculture, this stewardess had been a pretty sight for Dudung's eyes, which always sparkled because of his anemia (to be honest his blood was not good because he did not eat enough!). Dudung scolded himself, as he knew that a smile like that was unfair, tantamount to a billboard.

Instead he looked out the window, down at the natural beauty of West Java with its paddy fields bathed in the light of the morning sun, with the clouds drifting over beautiful Indonesia.

Now in the middle of this dark rainy night, Dudung was just reminiscing.

The one whose sandal had fallen off was fresh like the female doctor who injected him with B12 every week for his liver. He had been given a prescription for vitamins. Those two women—the stewardess and the doctor—were human beings swarming before his blood-deprived sparkling eyes. And now there were these two young chicks cheeping desolately as they scratched around in that pitch black night.

If those two young girls were given the right education, of course they would become stewardesses or doctors. But for the moment it was just their faces which made them look like that stewardess and that doctor!

And who's fault was that? In fact if one were to follow the chain of logic, the line would stand out, roaring like the sound of an engine. Maybe it was just like the Jatiluhur Dam! If water was provided efficiently by the Jatiluhur dam, then the yield of the fields would be plentiful. Not like now when many of the rice fields lie fallow and there is only one harvest per year. Jatiluhur was made years ago, but we are still waiting for the pipes to be installed. What are our leaders doing?

There is no attention being paid to small businesses in the villages, so the inhabitants depend entirely on the rice crop. They sell rice to buy their clothes, their homes, their furniture and their tools, and in the end they run out of rice. Finally young girls like these turn out like chicks cheeping in the night for food!

Look at those kids sitting behind him. They cannot be more than fourteen or fifteen years old. But they already go out at night with their faces powdered and their lips smeared with red to stop motorbikes and prostitute themselves. Believe it or not, seen from a financial point of view, they have no value. A pack of triple-five cigarettes would be of more importance to a driver who had dropped his cigarettes on the road. Seen from a financial point of view, these two girls had the same value as Dudung himself. The same as a saucepan to cook porridge for a corrupt man's baby.

No, no. They are after all, human beings. Ours is a nation of farmers. They are young female farmers just seeking a bit of additional income by enjoying the vehicles that can be bought with the yield of their crops.

"Haaakh!"

All at once Dudung's voice boomed out ten times louder than the engine of the motorbike.

The fields and the frogs, the crickets and the rice trembled in fear at such a sound. The two young girls were also afraid.

"Thanks you, sir, just stop here please."

"But why do you want to stop in the middle of these lonely fields?"

"We're afraid of you, sir, bellowing like that, like a drunk."

"So what are you going to do, just sit here on your own with the frogs and the crickets?'

"We're women, aren't we, we'll easily be able to stop another vehicle."

"OK, OK."

That night Dudung drank coffee in a village between Karawang and Bekasi. He was very tired. Once he had eaten in the little food stall, he slept on a bamboo bench until daybreak. When he woke up it was already light but the sun had not yet risen.

The two ladies of the night had become ladies of daylight, and in fact their home was not far from where Dudung had slept. They no longer recognized Dudung, which gave him the opportunity to observe what they were doing—among other things, saying their prayers, tidying the house and garden, fetching water from the well, looking after their younger siblings, and washing the clothes and the dishes. Now they were normal women by day!

They really did not recognize Dudung. For them he could have been a tree, a tire, an electricity pylon, any number of the things of the night. Yes, they were bits of flesh scattered between Karawang and Bekasi, not belonging to you.

And when the sun came up Dudung felt even more lonely, spinning on his wheels.

Between Beirut and Bali

There was a gentle breeze that morning. The sea lapped at the white sand bathed in the morning light. A few tourists were already out sunbathing and reading their books as I strolled past them looking for a small guesthouse facing the white sand and the open sea.

My God! It's as if she were a celestial being suddenly appearing before me on this beach so soon after what happened. Last week, as I was on my way back from Paris to have a holiday after a month working in the war zone in Beirut, I met her in Singapore. She said she was flying out to Bangkok, but here she was lying on the white sands of Sanur Beach. I tried to avoid her, but she beat me to it and quickly recognized me.

She strode towards me and tugged at me from behind as I turned away from her, then she pulled me down to sit in the sand. Her body was white and tall like a giraffe, something I did not like about her. But actually overall she had a good figure and a pretty face. Initially when I saw her swimming in the hotel where we were both staying in Singapore, I was attracted by the harmony of her body and by how pretty she was, but then when I realized that she was taller than me I lost interest. When we had a slight disagreement, I made it into a big thing, so she decided to fly off to Bangkok. Damn! And now there she was relaxing on the white sands of Sanur Beach just as I was wandering along looking for someone in a cottage on that beach.

"When did you arrive from Jakarta?" she asked.

"Last night," I answered.

"Where are you staying?"

"Nowhere. As you know, I can't sleep at night so I stayed up until morning," I said. "Then I bathed in the river and came straight here," I added.

"Oh, poor boy," she said in English. "When we were together in Singapore, I told you that you're basically lonely. And you're sick. You dream of a heaven full of women who treasure their own virginity and you keep dreaming about them," she said in a loud voice.

"Shut up!" I snapped, as her loud voice was disturbing the tourists nearby who were trying to read their books. "What are you reading, Amanda?" I asked, calling her by her name.

"A collection of sermons by a priest from Indonesia but written in English," she told me.

"Where are you staying?" I asked her.

"There, Ibu Murni's cottage," she said.

"Oh, that's the one I was looking for!" I said, pulling her up, and we went together to Ibu Murni's guesthouse.

How unfortunate. Amanda stuck close to me and I felt very awkward.

It was just a simple guesthouse, but this is what tourists from all around the world loved. In fact it wasn't just one hut but five or six of them, made of the wood and fronds of coconut palms. Even the walls were made of coconut leaves. Everything made of coconut material, as the guesthouse was under the palm trees.

We were greeted by an old woman in a sort of cute lobby area decorated with Balinese paintings and statues.

"I've brought you a letter from Rukmini in Paris, ma'am," I said.

On hearing the name of her daughter who was living in Paris, the woman beamed from ear to ear. "Yes, but how did you meet my

Rukmini? Are you living with her in Paris?" asked the old woman who still looked strong despite her years.

"No, ma'am, I work in the war zone in Beirut, and after finishing my work I was having a vacation in Paris. I met your daughter at our embassy there," I explained briefly.

"Oh, that makes me so happy. Tell me about yourself and what work you do that gets you mixed up in all these wars," said the woman. "Come and sit down."

Amanda was making the woman look at us both, as this "giraffe" was sitting right up close to me, hugging me with her big arm.

"I love it when a short little Indonesian man has a big tall foreign wife," said the old woman.

"Why, ma'am?"

Ibu Murni didn't answer me, as she had turned her attention to her daughter's letter which she had just taken out of the envelope. She read the letter, and we watched her face as it lit up with a smile as she read. I leaned against Amanda's sweaty, sandy body.

"Thank you, thank you, she's just telling me about the money she's sent from Paris and how she and her husband are leaving for Kuwait, as he's working as a doctor there," said the woman, looking up. "Eh, I nearly forgot to answer your question, son," she said. "Yes, you're a good match. Later your children will be tall and probably will grow up to be volleyball players or boxers or football players. Indonesians can never become really good football players unless they're the offspring of couples like you that produce big tall children!" said the woman, smiling with happiness.

"We're not married yet, ma'am," I said in English.

"We met in Singapore," said Amanda.

"I just got here last night," I said.

"Where are you staying?" asked Ibu Murni.

"Here," stated Amanda firmly.

I held my breath.

"Now you two are my guests. I'm going to make breakfast for you both," said Ibu Murni telephoning through to the kitchen staff.

"So, son, you're fighting in the war in Beirut? So Indonesian soldiers are fighting in Beirut, are they?" asked Ibu Murni.

"No, ma'am. If anyone's a soldier, it's Amanda," I said jokingly. Amanda smiled. "This guy is very amusing. He picked me up in Singapore with his cheekiness."

"I'm only small but I can still pick up a giraffe, ma'am!" I said.

The old woman laughed and laughed, then added, "But don't be like that. This young woman will give birth to big Indonesian children who will become football players and make our country proud."

"Do you like watching football, ma'am?" I asked.

"No, my late husband was the one who loved football. He was a football player, a coach, and organized football matches. When he got too old to play football and all that, he became a sports columnist," said Ibu Murni in English. She always spoke English whenever she looked in our direction and saw Amanda and me sitting right next to one another.

"Maybe your husband was big and tall," I said.

"Actually, no. And that's something he complained about all his life. Why, why was it that Indonesians had such small bodies? And because of that he encouraged Rukmini to marry a big tall man so that his grandchildren would be big and tall, too. Rukmini chose a big tall European, but unfortunately they don't have any children," she said with a look of unfulfilled yearning.

"Sorry," I said. "Our conversation has strayed off the original subject, ma'am."

"I already told this guy that I wanted to have a child with him, but in Singapore we had a fight over something small and it was all off," said Amanda.

"I would look after that child myself, or Rukmini. They both want to adopt a child," said Ibu Murni.

I looked at Amanda wide-eyed with astonishment. "If the child's *bulé* [European-looking] you just take him and send him to Rukmini," I said jokingly. "If the child is mulatto-looking and is big and tall, Amanda can take him, as I'm afraid the child will always stick up for his mother."

"Ah, we have the imagination," said Amanda. "But the important thing is whether we have the will. I've already told this Indonesian man that I have savings and am ready to stop working and would like to live on a big piece of land beside a beautiful lake or beach, with plenty of fish. I'm sure I could have several children with this Indonesian," said Amanda.

"What noble, holy sentiments. I'll be alongside you both if those sentiments can be realized," said the older woman, whose age must have been around sixty.

The food had already been prepared under the shade of the trees on the beach, and we went out to have breakfast there.

That day Amanda and I spent a lot of time swimming in the sea and then rested in the guesthouse until nightfall. After dinner we were so sleepy that we did not have a chance to chat with Ibu Murni. The night was very quiet. There just was the sound of the waves breaking on the beach and the night breeze was very cool, so we slept soundly.

In the middle of the night there was a knock at the door. Amanda staggered to the door and opened it. It was Ibu Murni.

"Amanda, you've forgotten. It's already time," said Ibu Murni.

"Oh, sorry. It's all this Indonesian man's fault," said Amanda.

Hearing these words in my tired sleepy state, I felt a mixture of astonishment and irritation. I left the two of them to it and fell back onto my pillow. Maybe just a few seconds later I was fast asleep again, until at some point in time from afar I heard people singing and weeping. I sat up with my heart beating hard. I wasn't aware of anything around me, as I was concentrating on the strange things I could hear. When the singing stopped, I heard the sound of people praying. I concluded that it was those two women.

I walked slowly in their direction. In a dining room in the same building as our bedroom, I saw the two of them kneeling and praying with fervor. When I saw that, I went back to the bedroom, took my cigarettes, and went to smoke at a dining table at the far end. The two of them prayed for a long time, prayers mixed with moans and poignant words of remorse and requests for forgiveness of all their sins. I was no longer sleepy, and I was not even aware that I had smoked three cigarettes.

Suddenly I witnessed a new spectacle. A number of black cats came in from the garden, jumped up onto the table, and sat looking calmly at the two women praying. They were all very black with a sharp look in their eyes. There were about seven of them. It was kind of cool just watching those cats sitting quietly as if they were joining in the prayers.

Damn! Suddenly a white cat with five little kittens jumped up onto another of the tables. Did they want to pray too? Who knows. They just sat there quietly. Then all at once they looked up at the roof of the hut made of palm fronds. There among the bamboo rafters were several mice scampering around and looking down. All the cats on the table just looked up at them quietly. Strange. They did not try and climb up the posts to attack them. I laughed to myself as I watched that. Maybe the war between the cats and the mice would only begin once the lady of the house had finished praying.

The two women—whose words of prayer flowed without a break, while I smoked my seven cigarettes—suddenly began singing softly but freely. That marked the end of their long midnight prayer session. Once they had finished, all the cats began to move. They all jumped down and ran to their mistress. I noticed that even the mice were running along the bamboo rafters and down to the ground.

Ibu Murni was busy. She opened the cupboard and took out two food trays. The first one, which was quite big, she filled with food for the cats, and the second smaller one with food for the mice. She put the two trays down next to each other and soon I witnessed the most extraordinary sight. The mice and cats began to eat side by side and did not bother one another. There were a few naughty ones who were biting each other, but when the old woman scolded them they were quiet again. Once the two food trays were empty, the animals went away.

"It's usually like that. Whenever I pray like that in the middle of the night, all God's creatures are waiting. They're like my children," said the old woman, her eyes tired but smiling.

"Where have they gone?" I asked.

"They'll be sitting quietly listening to the sound of the crickets and the frogs in the pond. Oh, I need to feed the frogs and the fish, they're waiting!" said the old woman as, with limbs stiff with rheumatism, she made her way slowly to another cupboard and took out food for the frogs.

In the middle of the night we proceeded to the pond, which was full of water lilies. As we approached, my goodness, the sound of the frogs got more and more animated. They nearly all leapt into the pool, lit up by garden lamps. The old woman sprinkled the food on the surface of the pond, which became a flurry of movement of frogs and fish.

I felt a great happiness seeing all this, but at the same time a concern that all this was happening because of human solitude. Among all God's creatures, the human being was the one who was most able to overcome loneliness, but at the same time was the most susceptible to loneliness unless he made certain choices. This old woman had made her choice.

But above all I felt happy that Amanda had found real friendship with this older woman, a friend who accompanied her in prayer so that she did not feel alone in this big wide world. Amanda was like me. She flew around from country to country and everywhere she felt a sense of loneliness, especially in the big cities. She was like you, sometimes feeling very lonely in the city concrete jungles, and even more so sitting alone on a flight or in a soulless hotel room in some skyscraper.

I felt very guilty when on our last night she decided to continue her journey to Bangkok and then on to Tokyo to start a new contract. Why did I have to leave a woman who had told me from her heart that she really loved me?

"Let's get married in Australia or just in Singapore," I said.

"Why?"

"So that our relationship is on a legal footing. Who knows, if we have a child, that child has a legal basis on which to claim his or her inheritance," I said.

"Whatever. I will leave my destiny in the hands of God," said Amanda as she drifted into sleep.

We had breakfast under the trees facing the beach and the sea. Both dressed in our swimsuits. Suddenly my food stuck in my throat when a Balinese woman carrying sarongs for sale on her head approached Amanda. There were four small children with her, also carrying sarongs, paintings, statues, and other souvenirs.

I stood up and chased them away. In Balinese I told them that there was no point in trying to sell their stuff to this tall *bulé* woman because she did not have any money. I insisted that they went away and then we sat on a low stone wall under a *waru* tree.

"Nyoman, your third-born, is dead!" said the Balinese woman.

"What was wrong with him?" I asked, feeling as if I had been struck by lightning.

"He fell from a coconut tree!" said the woman.

I had to pull myself together quickly. "Later I'll come home. Just carry on selling your stuff at that hotel over there. There're lots of tourists there. I've still got a lot of things to sort out with the boss. I just got back from Beirut last night and I had to work late into the night," I said, kissing the children, two girls and two boys, who had stopped going to school so that they could help their mother sell stuff on the beach.

"Siregaaaaar! Finish your breakfast!" shouted Amanda, calling my name musically.

I went back to Amanda's table. Out of the corner of my eye, I watched my wife carrying her wares surrounded by her four children, all barefoot and with their hair bleached by the sun and the sea breezes. I took a deep breath. It was a big blow which had struck me deep in my soul. I felt very troubled by a sense of guilt.

"Who was that woman and those children?" asked Amanda.

I did not answer her immediately. "War reporters like me wage internal wars, too," I said.

"Who were they?" she asked again.

"My wife. She told me that my third-born son died when he fell from a coconut tree. Anyway. It's my own fault. While I spent the last five years travelling around the world, I never sent them any money."

"No wonder you said last night that we would get married in Singapore or Australia. No wonder. Because you're still not divorced from your wife here in Bali. No wonder," said Amanda. "But you're really mean never sending money home for your children so they're forced to hang around on the beach selling souvenirs!" she shouted. "You just waste your money in night clubs and sleep with the striptease artists!" said Amanda raising her voice even more.

"Yes, with striptease artists like the one in front of me," I said.

Amanda kept quiet. She shook her head. "I've learned my lesson, my dear Siregar," she said. "I need to take you back to your wife and I'll take care of the cats, the mice and the frogs with Ibu Murni."

Woven Cloth

Once the whaling boat had gone out to sea, Anna would begin her routine work. The routine tasks that she needed to complete were quite manageable, as it was not yet the planting season and the harvesting season was already behind them. Her routine work consisted of going two or three times a week to some bushy thickets on the slope of the hill to collect firewood, then cooking for her four children, who went to school at a Catholic mission situated on the side of an infertile rocky hill of coral. After finishing all that, Anna would go out under the coconut, banana, areca, candlenut, and almond trees to make a start on the task that she considered most sacred. She would weave a cloth with the most beautiful designs to be worn on Christmas Day, which would be upon them in just a few months' time.

To do her weaving, Anna would sit on a mat spread out on the sand, breathing in the sea breeze cooled by the filter of the leaves of the trees. Her ears were not conscious of the sound of the waves, and yet that sound automatically moved her hands as they pulled on the threads again and again, supple hands which threaded the yarn in and out. She felt a sense of great happiness to be moving whatever needed to be moved. Her very soul was immersed in a secret happiness accompanied by the sound of the sea. She felt very happy whenever the whaling boat went out to sea. It had already become routine that her husband had to go out to sea to catch whales and that he would come home bringing those giant fish to share with the whole village and the small island of Lembata.

The same went for her children. They were part of the blissful existence on this little island. Every morning they would go to school, every afternoon they would come home and play with the areca and candlenuts on the road or in the clean white sand yard, or they would climb the barren hill, looking for pieces of charcoal from the *kesambi* trees burnt by the dry-season fires—fires which would eat up the hillsides when the dry season arrived. Then the children would carry the charcoal home to be used to cook fish and vegetables and to roast cassava and breadfruit. When Anna's children climbed those barren hills of Lembata Island, they would always look out to sea, looking for dots on the horizon far away. And if those cute fresh-faced creatures saw that there was an isolated dot floating alone right out on the horizon as far as the eye could see, then they would jump up and down happily shouting: "That's Father, that's Father, oh Father, Father's watching with his radar. What he's set his heart on is a whale bigger than any that's ever been caught on this island of ours."

The children were very happy and proud of their father. Although their father did not own a boat and all the fishing tackle—although their father was not the skipper of his own craft—their father was said to be a brave fisherman. He was the one who did everything. He was the man who plunged his spear into the flank of the whale, then would "walk" the whale hanging on to the strap attached to the spear, then would plunge his spear deeper into the very heart of the fish. If the whale got frightened and swam away pulling the boat behind it, it was the father of Anna's children who was brave enough to hang on and "walk" the whale back to the boat. Dozens of whales had already been brought to their shores, and they had heard scores of stories about the bravery of their father. To the point where they no longer considered all this as anything special. They had simply absorbed it all into their picture of the world as children. And they slept and awoke each morning with a sense of happiness.

Usually, when the children came home from school, they just threw down the firewood which they had brought from the hillside, then looked for something to eat in the kitchen. They never bothered their mother when she was weaving. Before they went out to play with the areca nuts and candlenuts, the children were accustomed to asking their mother if she was thirsty. And whenever she said she was thirsty, they climbed up and got her a young coconut, and only then went out to play in the playground of their games with the areca nuts and candlenuts. Anna's children were very clever at playing games with areca nuts and candlenuts. If they won, they would get, not just five or ten nuts, but half or even a whole sack of candlenuts. They would sell their winnings and give the money to their mother.

Anna's husband had already been out at sea for a long time. She accepted it as normal, although deep in her heart it caused her suffering. "If that happens to me again in my lifetime, I will surrender the rest of my life to God." That was how her heart responded. Her hands still went on working the loom, her hands still went on intertwining one thread with another. And yet, beneath all that, after her husband had already been out on the open seas searching for whales for a month, Anna's soul began to weave anxiety and hope desolately, as expansive as the open sea and as dry as the coral hills of Lembata.

Every morning, as she waited for her husband to return, her soul murmured in rhythm with her destiny in the tapping of the loom, in the sound of the waves on the beach. Ah! These sounds were sending her secret messages from the middle of the ocean, from which point, from where on the horizon, heaven only knows. Tired, Anna took a deep breath, and stopped muttering to herself.

Then she continued again. Nobody knew the language of life which was woven within her. Inner thread after inner thread had been woven by experience, by the arid hills of Lembata, by the sea, and by two marriages which had produced children. This was indeed a strange inner tapestry. In the village they always used threads made from cotton dipped in dyes of the colors of the island, then made it into woven cloth with the designs of Lembata, but within oneself there was a weaving which was even more beautiful, the determination Anna received from the stillness and desolation of the sea, from this small island with its arid hills.

After her husband had gone, she began to take deep breaths and with each breath she retrieved threads of memory which she had already woven deep into her soul. The first born was a boy who was given to her by a courageous whale fisherman. After her husband (the father of her first child) had speared ten whales, he had an accident, was seriously wounded at sea and, still a mere youth, his body was transported back to Lembata. It was a huge blow to Anna, who was still young. While the people flocked down to the sea to receive their good fortune from the sea, while the people brought their hatchets and machetes and were busy dividing up the flesh, whale bones and oil, Anna who was still so young surrendered herself to her grief. She used a woven blanket—which she had made when she had been crowned the prettiest young girl of the beach—to wrap her husband's corpse in, then she sat in the clothes which she had woven herself while they accompanied his body with prayers in the church, right until this young sailor was buried in his native soil in Lembata, the island that was always buffeted by the sea breeze and the Spirit of Christ.

Anna got through her mourning period with determination, busy as she was with the birth of her first child, then taking good care of him until he no longer required breast-feeding. After that she organized herself with the work that was most fitting to a woman—

that is, weaving—weaving colorful blankets with local designs. She no longer had time to think about the tragedy of her husband and her fatherless child, because she already felt comforted. Whatever it was that fate had dealt her, it was not without consequence. Everything gave new inner strength, determination, and faith. She became ever more devoted to her prayers, whether at home or at church. She grew closer and closer to Mother Mary.

One day, when she was taking her woven cloth to the market, something happened that would change the course of her life. She was sitting next to a young man who was selling smoked whale meat. The market was very busy. Many dugouts and boats had arrived from other small islands and villages, and among them was a gentleman wearing boots who had also come to do his shopping. This gentleman was well-built and had a rough voice. "Hey, how much is that salt fish?" he asked, indicating which one he meant with his boot. The big gentleman then proceeded to indicate lots of the chunks of smoked whale meat with his boot. Confused, this young man from the arid island—this local whale challenger— became offended.

"Sir, this is food, not bat shit. Why are you pointing to it with your foot? If you want, just step on it first then eat it!" said the young man.

The gentleman in boots also got offended. "What? Don't you know the customer is king?"

"But a stupid king you are, sir!" said the young man. "The leather that covers your foot, sir, is not edible. What's the matter with you! This fish is highly nutritious and you don't have to go looking for it far from your own country, like your imported shoes that you bought with a lot of Indonesian money," said the young man who was not wearing any shoes, but was well-built because he often ate smoked whale meat, which was full of vitamins and nutrients.

"Ah! So you know everything, do you! Like you've been to school!" he said.

"I've had my share of schooling. Graduate of that Catholic junior high school over there!" said the young man. "Then I became a fisherman."

The man in boots felt that this young man was insulting him. He felt his authority was being undermined by the words of this simple fisherman. The gentleman drew back his arm and slapped him on the face several times.

The young man kept quiet.

But Anna's heart would not keep quiet. She shuddered as she remembered her uncle's experience at the time of the Dutch. Once a Dutch policeman had come to the market and had rudely stepped on the cassava that her uncle had spread out on the ground in the market. Her uncle protested, but the policeman kicked all his cassava. "Hey, don't block the way!" said the Dutch policeman. The uncle's cassava was flung away like so many balls. Then one Sunday morning, while that very policeman was fishing on the beach, Anna's uncle approached him with his machete unsheathed.

Very strange! On that little island, one's self-esteem was more important than any other value that could come and go. Policemen come and go, shoes come and go, but one's self-esteem may never be insulted. The man who carried that machete was certain that sacred food had been kicked by shoes that had been bought in a shop. Why were imported products thought to be better than things produced from the local soil, produced with the sweat of hard work, and work that was a limb of this life?

That Dutch policeman had insulted their food, insulted their productive work. Deep inside, Anna's uncle felt that producing food for other human beings was a sacred task, so he was offended. He got mad. Very strange. So one Sunday her uncle took his machete and approached the Dutch policeman, who enjoying his time off fishing, standing in the surf with the waves lapping at his feet. While the policeman was happily catching fish which were flapping around, glistening like silver, at that moment Anna's uncle pulled out his machete and plunged it into the neck of that Dutch policeman. The policeman turned around, pulled out a gun, and aimed it at her uncle's heart. Both died tragically with the waves lapping at their bodies.

Anna remembered all that very well. How horrible! Anna was horrified at her village people's character, which preferred to settle every disagreement with the machete. She wondered why the inhabitants of this arid little island full of whalers were so hot-tempered. Oh! She had to save that young man selling the smoked whale meat!

Late at night the forsaken widow, Anna, dressed neatly in a sarong she had woven herself, and took a candle to the statue of Mother Mary to pray. "O, Mother Mary. The Mother who gave birth to a Son who has so much love for all humanity, even his enemies. Petrus, the young sailor, is beside himself with anger and wants to take revenge on that man with the boots he bought in a Chinese shop. Please pray for him! Pray to your Son that he may send the Holy Spirit to Petrus so that he does not end up committing murder!"

That same night, with a blanket she had just finished weaving, which she wrapped up with twine made from the flowers of the areca nut, she set off towards the hut where the young fisherman Petrus lived. The sea breeze was rustling in the leaves of the thatched roof as she stooped and entered the hut. There, as she had suspected, was Petrus sharpening his machete in the light of a coconut oil lamp.

"Petrus!" called Anna in a flat voice. "What are you doing with that machete?"

"Nothing!" said Petrus.

"Do you want to wind up like all those murderers on Nusa Kambangan?"

'Shut up, woman!" growled Petrus.

Anna made the sign of the cross. Petrus stared at her as he continued to sharpen his machete. But notwithstanding, in that second his glance touched her very soul. She felt suddenly disturbed. But, oh! The flow of revenge in someone who has been offended is stronger than the blade of a machete which has just been sharpened. A thumb can indeed feel the sharpness of a blade. "Hair which has grown wild can be cut, let alone a person who is arrogant because of his shoes!" he said standing up and putting the machete inside the sarong hanging on his back. "Why have you come here in the dead of night, Anna?" asked Petrus "What will people say?"

"For the sake of Mother Mary, I beseech you not to take revenge like my uncle did, just because of some shoes," said Anna.

"Revenge? What's revenge?" asked Petrus.

"Don't kill the man who offended you with his shoes. Be patient. Be patient, and flames will descend upon the head of your enemy," said Anna. "You're still young. Better take advantage of your youth on this island. The children and the island inhabitants living in the interior still need fish, the rich nutritious whale meat. Here's a sarong for you which I wove myself. Put it on nicely and go and pray in the church." She put the sarong on the bed.

That night Petrus changed. In the days that followed, something happened that was more than the change that had taken place that night. While that night Petrus stopped wanting to kill that man with the boots who had insulted their sacred food, in the following days he fell in love with Anna. Later the two of them received the sacrament of marriage on one of the hills there.

The marriage between the two of them was full of happiness and they had three children. Add to that the child from Anna's first marriage, Petrus had to work hard as a sailor on a whaling boat to put food on the table for his four children and their mother.

That was Anna, and that was Petrus. Now Petrus had been out at sea for a long time. But Anna was certain that the whale he had speared was a big one and full of resistance. Usually a whale like that would pull the boat off around the Sabu Sea, towards the waters of the islands of Timor, Sumba, and Flores. Had that fish taken them off to the Indonesian Ocean, and then on to Madagascar or the waters of Australia? mused Anna. "Oh, just forget about it!" She cheered herself up. "He'll come back."

Anna just got on with her weaving. Anna just cooked for her children who were still at school. The first year had already passed, then the second, the third, the fourth and the fifth. Petrus did not come home, nor did his best friend from among all the whalers. It was clear that their boat had sunk to the bottom of the Sabu Sea or in the Indonesian Ocean.

Anna was already an old woman when her first son married a young girl who was a skilled weaver. Now the two of them weave together under the shade of the banana, areca, and coconut trees, with the waves lapping nearby, while her son goes out to sea with a new whaling boat.

Anna weaves for the grandchild who will be born to her daughter-in-law who is now pregnant, while her daughter-in-law weaves for her husband, the son of Anna, the brave young sailor.

When the Jackfruit Tree Was Bearing Fruit

That day was a Sunday. I was sitting under a jackfruit tree in the garden in front of my house. Right then the tree had lots of fruit on it, big ones and small ones. The big ones were hanging at the base of the tree, not far off the ground, but there were also big heavy ones higher up waiting to ripen.

I was busy taking pictures with my automatic camera, sitting beside the fruit of my jackfruit tree, clicking away, then standing up, more clicks, then getting up onto a small ladder facing a big branch, sitting up there with my legs hanging down, then...

"Ugh, Father, what an eccentric old man you are. If you fall, you'll break a leg. What with you being so stiff and rheumatic and all..."

The voice belonged to my youngest child, a teenage girl who was in her second year in high school.

"Come down!" she told me, holding onto the ladder.

I climbed down smiling at my daughter.

"Sorry, child, but I'm just so proud of this jackfruit tree. And just look at those breadfruit trees over there. Look, they've all got fruit on them. In a few weeks we'll be able to enjoy bread made from breadfruit. Look!" I said to my daughter who really did care about her father's welfare.

"But please don't go climbing trees anymore, Dad, OK?" she advised.

"OK, OK. I won't do that anymore. I'll just sit and read. Will you make me another coffee please? With milk!" I said, picking up my book by the Japanese writer, Ryunosuke Akutagawa, entitled *Rashomon*.

From the dining room there wafted the sound of a famous traditional Sundanese singer (*pesinden*) that we loved listening to. In that house lived only three of God's creatures—a father, his son who was currently studying at University, and his sweet daughter who really loved her father. My oldest child was an agricultural engineer and lived in one of the transmigration regions. There he had quite a big piece of land and had planted all kinds of crops. It goes without saying that he has his talent for farming from me, but now I find myself asking him lots of questions. As my health is not so good these days and because my younger son is still studying in Jakarta, I could not go with him to farm in the transmigration region. I was instructed to look after our home in Jakarta and cultivate our garden, which is fairly large by Jakarta standards.

Living in Jakarta is quite safe. I have easy access to the best doctors and hospitals and the best university is not far away. From time to time my oldest son comes to see us and to visit his mother's grave. The children are very proud of the fact that their mother is buried in the heroes' cemetery. Yes indeed, my wife was a female hero in the Revolution. She had quite a few bullets nestling in her body, which were removed surgically by a doctor. Perhaps because of her heroism my beloved wife did not spend very long on this earth.

As a man I tended to choose to play the role of father rather than mother. But this choice was not an easy one. For in fact while I was fulfilling the dual roles of mother and father, I once met a woman. Ah, but I try not to think about her and all that in my old age...

The sound of the *pesinden*'s voice wafted out of the dining room. My teenage daughter liked to listen to this music while she worked. But I found it distracting and my concentration was gone, so I laid my book aside and just let myself be cradled by the sound of the Sundanese *kecapi* [stringed instrument] and the voice of the *pesinden*.

One night when Jakarta was already free of the tumult of thousands of cars, I could not sleep. My children, who were still young, had all fallen sound asleep. Back then when my wife was still alive, I did not get so restless. But when my eldest son started studying at ITB and lived in Bandung, I felt more and more lonely. Usually I just stayed at home taking the night air, looking at the stars and conversing secretly with my wife. I recalled that long period of the Revolution, when my wife became a spy and went into the Dutch camps disguised as a village woman. She disguised herself as a *pesinden*, as a domestic servant, and, oh no, I don't even want to think about what else. I just wanted to get drowsy so that I could go back to sleep. So I went for a walk to make myself tired and sleepy. But I didn't get sleepy. So that night I went into the little streets and alleyways of a market area, which was quite lively, as the vegetable sellers had brought in vegetables from the Pasar Induk fruit and vegetable market and were busy buying and selling.

I continued along a dark alley. Here the verandas of the Chinese stores were bustling with people silhouetted in the dark as they moved around in all directions. It was somehow touching. And all the more so with the sound of the voice of a *pesinden*, I was more in a pocket of night life than an ordinary night. I was in a state of meaningless solitude and like them moved around like a silhouette in the night, activated by the voice of the singer.

I walked towards the sound of that voice. A woman was sitting humming beside a blind masseur, who was reclining smoking a cigarette and cocking his head with unseeing eyes, and the other, the *pesinden*, was singing. When she saw me she asked, "Do you want a massage, sir?" On hearing that, the blind man patted his

mat as a sign that he was offering his services as a masseur. Without
further delay, I surrendered my aching body to the solitude of this
night world accompanied by the sound of the Sundanese singer.

I sprawled out on the mat in my underpants. I lay face down
using my arms as a pillow, and the masseur began to press his
thumbs into the part of my leg which was giving me pain. Oh,
what pleasure!

As I enjoyed the massage, the blind man asked, "Don't you
want a pillow, sir?"

"Where's there a pillow?" I asked

"I have one."

"If you have one, yes please. As long as it's clean."

"Yes, it's clean."

All at once I felt my head being lifted up as if I were a pampered
child and placed in the lap of the singer. I was taken aback by
the strong smell of the batik cloth she was wearing. I took a deep
breath. So this was how these creatures earned a living. All these
silhouettes on the verandas of the Chinese shops, where were they
all heading? And me just sprawled out on my own, lost in my own
thoughts.

"Where are you from, miss?" I asked my pillow.

"From Indramayu."

I did not want to ask her any more questions. All Indonesians
know that this area is a wasteland. A wasteland of rice fields! In the
rainy season the rice fields are extensive, so why is it then that so
many pretty girls from Indramayu end up in Jakarta as prostitutes
or butterflies of the night? Probably because that area is indeed
a wasteland of rice fields. The people there should plant other
things apart from rice, like breadfruit, jackfruit, and other sorts
of fruit. I would prefer to see this area planted with sago and fruit
trees, so that all sorts of animals and insects, including bees, would
come, and there would be millions of types of trees, which would

yield fruit and wood to give the people a source of income. They shouldn't just keep planting rice and rice only. Perhaps the pretty women of my nation are proud of this monoculture. And among them was my pillow here. Oh God! This soulful song stems from the depths of this culture of rice-field wasteland!

This was how I daydreamed.

After my massage I invited this pretty woman to have dinner in a Padang restaurant. There I proposed to her right away. She accepted my proposal and a few weeks later we got married in Indramayu. I built a simple house on her father's land, calculating that if my children came to know that they had a stepmother, this stepmother was not just a silhouette of the night which could metamorphose into the masseur's pillow on the veranda of the shop. I believed that all human beings could change. Being a night silhouette or a pillow were just different manifestations of the imperative to make a living. All human beings had hidden within themselves the possibility of being good people, even if they had already metamorphosed into a prostitute. Although this traditional singer, who provided entertainment at village parties, was a pretty woman who had been promiscuous, she had the potential to make a good wife. And in truth, several months after our marriage, she had become a really good woman. She opened a food stall and worked hard to make her business a success.

One day she got on a bus and came to Jakarta to introduce herself to my children, who were all waiting for her. But all at once came the news that there had been a collision between two long distance buses. Dozens of people had been killed, among them my pretty wife...

"Father, Father!" called my son. "Don't sleep like that out in the wind. You'll get another chill!"

"No," I said. "I wasn't asleep. I was just daydreaming and gazing at my jackfruit trees laden with fruit. Aren't they beautiful?"

My son who was studying at university was standing beside me, accompanied by a pretty young woman. "And who's this?" I asked.

"She's my friend and she's studying to be a doctor," he said. "Apparently her father is an old friend of yours from the same village."

"Oh, what's his name?" I asked.

"My father's called Leo," said the young woman.

"Leo, yes, Leo…" I remembered this Leo very well indeed; but, as I stood out there under my jackfruit tree, I was taken aback by how his daughter had met my son like this. "Come on, let's go inside and find your sister. She's probably preparing something to eat," I said.

Once the two youngsters had gone inside, I reverted to being an old man full of memories and nostalgia. When I returned to our village some years ago, I saw that Leo had become a rich man. He owned extensive coffee and coconut plantations. No wonder he was able to put his daughter through medical school in Jakarta. No wonder. But between Leo and me there was a hidden secret which still caused me pain in my heart and in my treasure trove of memories. It was complicated to talk about this to anyone and difficult to get rid of these feelings. I felt very awkward about coming face to face with this rich man called Leo, as I thought that he would inevitably feel disturbed if he met me. If he did meet me, I'm sure that he would be embarrassed by the "goodness" I would show towards him. The story went like this.

When Leo and I were small, our lives were deeply affected by the world war and the struggle for independence. It goes without saying that those were hard times. Leo's parents were illiterate peasants who did not have any fertile land on which they could grow corn, cassava, or rice. The soil on their land was very poor, and although they strove to make it more fertile with green compost made of different plants and weeds, they produced only a little

cassava and hardly any corn. So because of this I used to take Leo
with me to my fields to harvest corn, pumpkins, and cassava. Our
rice crop was ripening so we were busy harvesting it. Leo and his
parents helped us with the harvesting and were given a quarter of
the total yield.

As we worked away busily, I realized that the skinny little boy,
Leo, who never got enough to eat, was not there. I called him
and called him, I went looking for him everywhere, but he had
disappeared. In the end I stopped looking for him, as I thought he
had maybe gone fishing down at the river. I turned to the right of
the hut to get a drink of water. As I opened the door of the hut,
I saw Leo stealing rice and the delicious fish that my mother had
cooked. I saw that his mouth was so full of food that he could
hardly chew it. Oh my God! Probably because he was so afraid
of getting caught red-handed, he was swallowing the fish, bones
and all, and I was sure he would get one of those bones caught
in his throat. And his eyes were those of a frightened dog, even
though his jaws were working hard to finish chewing the stolen
food which he still had in his mouth. He observed me wide-eyed as
his jaws continued to chew. His gullet pushed the food down into
his stomach. His famished face and eyes and his thin little body
moved me to pity, and I resolved to quietly shut the door of the hut
again and leave him in peace to finish the food he had stolen. I did
not punish him. But what had happened must surely have made
him more aware and motivated him all his life to seek out the best
food on fertile soil.

In the end he established his own fertile lands. In the end the
skinny hungry little child who was once caught red-handed stealing
food became the king of coffee and coconuts. And his daughter
was studying medicine even though her father had been illiterate.
People's destiny turns out in so many different ways! And now this
daughter of his was my son's friend. Yes, a human being who was

once a thief can become a good person. Perhaps the journey of a human being from doing evil to doing good very much depends on how that person was treated when he was caught doing something bad. If back then I had caught him and beaten him black and blue, he might well have turned into a criminal or, even more extreme, have gone mad and would certainly not have produced a daughter who would go on to become a doctor.

I began thinking a lot about my wife. She started out as the pillow of a blind masseur, then became my clever wife who worked hard to open a food and drinks stall in her native Indramayu. But God had other plans for her. God took her back to be with him after she had married me and become a good woman. May she be sitting beside God in heaven in her after-life beyond.

Now Leo is as old as I am. We were both blessed with children. We both dedicated ourselves to growing things and producing crops we could trade. But there is a difference. In his old age Leo was wealthy with his extensive farm land and plantations, while I lived in the middle of a big city in a house with a modest garden. But my son had become a success like Leo. And besides he had become an agricultural engineer. In a few years Leo would be very happy when his daughter qualified as a doctor. Extraordinary! An illiterate man like him could have a daughter who became a doctor by virtue of his work opening up coffee and coconut plantations. If he had become a *becak* driver, then his daughter would probably have become a prostitute. Ah! Humans can only change by planting their land with different crops and by just planting rice....

"Father! Come in out of the wind. You'll get sick again..." said my youngest daughter as she brought me out a snack. That happened to me a lot. If I fell asleep outside I often caught a cold, unless I was careful.

"No," I said. "I was just daydreaming, thinking about that friend of your brother's. Her father is a good friend of mine," I added.

My youngest daughter whispered in my ear, "They've been going out for ages."

I raised my heavy eyebrows. Rather than living through my memories, I returned to the real world of the here and now.

Sandalwood Fans

I was all alone in the world. But I was still able to live adequately, in the sense that I was not dependent on anyone. I was able to eat three times a day and lived in a room which I rented. In that room there was a bed, a bathroom, and a kitchen. On the back veranda the roof protruded quite far out from the wall so I was able to keep the stove, the dish rack, the bucket, and the bicycle out there. In my room there was a second-hand television which entertained me every day.

If only my daughter had not married that man who works in the Middle East, maybe I would not have been alone, as my daughter would have been able to take care of me, and my two grandchildren would have kept me entertained. But fortunately at least my daughter helps provide for me. For a long time, when my wife was still alive, we had just enough to live on. On the back veranda, my wife would cook food that she could sell. Fish wrapped in banana leaves *(pepes)*, rice cooked in coconut (*nasi uduk*), roasted eggplant, and a spicy chilli sauce that I called "Sambal Inul Cili-cili." Every day I would travel around on my bike selling that food. I would peddle around from early morning till afternoon or even evening. The places I targeted to sell our food were the traditional market and building sites where there were laborers working.

But everything fell apart when my wife died. My daughter, who was in her first year in high school at the time, had to stop her schooling because she had to help me. Every night I had to cook what my wife had taught me. But then after I had finished cooking I needed to rest for a half a day, so we did not have the whole day to sell the food. Fortunately my daughter got to know a girl from Madura who sold *kue cucur*, fried cakes made of rice flour and sugar.

"Father, I want to be like that girl from Madura," said my daughter. "She dropped out of elementary school but she still managed to become a director."

"Ah, don't make me laugh," I said.

"All she needed as initial investment was a small stove and a pan for the rice flour batter. She's become a successful entrepreneur with her *kue cucur*. They're a real best seller, Father," said my daughter. "I want to be a *kue cucur* seller like her."

"But what about the food business handed down to you by your mother?" I said. "Will you have to give that up? Will the money you make be enough to feed both of us?"

"Easy. We just need a table. Some of the food you cook we'll put on the table and some of it you'll take around on your bike. OK?"

So three days later there was a table installed in the traditional market, laden with food, and beside it a sizzling stove which emitted the smell of frying rice-cakes. The girl from Madura, my daughter's *kue cucur* "mentor," sold her fare not far from my daughter's. Every morning at dawn my daughter would go off alone to sell her food at the traditional market. I would sleep until eleven o'clock, then I would ride my bike to the market, and pick up part of the food that my daughter was selling. Then I would peddle around the busy building sites, the fences outside factories, and other such places.

One day at dawn, a young journalist from the tabloid *Suara Pasar* [The Market Voice]—a young man who loved staying up all night talking—squatted down in front of my daughter's stove. This young journalist had fallen in love with my daughter. He put a big photo of my daughter and the girl from Madura in his newspaper.

The story in brief was all about the Small-scale Investment Program introduced by the New Order government, which made it easy for small-scale investors to get credit, a program which sank without a trace.

Then my daughter married that journalist from *Suara Pasar.* Her friend, the girl from Madura, was a bit down for a while until a few months later a taxi driver asked for her hand in marriage.

Not long afterwards, my son-in-law moved to the Middle East to work as a journalist on the magazine *Oil,* thanks to one of his uncles who worked in an oil company.

My daughter and son-in-law, however, could not help me much, because over there they were both studying while they worked. My son-in-law went to university and my daughter finished high school and went on to university, too.

But they could still help my financial circumstances. My daughter sent me money so I could buy sandalwood and agarwood fans that could be sold in the Middle East. And besides sandalwood fans, necklaces made of beads of sandalwood and agarwood. Then they asked me to send pieces of sandalwood and agarwood to sell to rich people for burning on their braziers.

And so this is how it came about that I was kept busy with my new business as a trader in sandalwood fans. Every month I sent off my fragrant merchandise. I rented a post box for this activity. Everything was on a small scale. A small post box, a small bedroom, and yet with this small venture I was able to connect with the big wide world! And although the sandalwood fan business went well enough for me to buy a piece of land in Jakarta, my daughter and her husband objected to me buying land to build a house in the city, as according to my daughter it would be destroyed by floods of water and floods of people.

To my mind, theirs was a strange way of thinking.

Whenever I went to the post office to send the merchandise, I would call in at a small food stall situated in the yard opposite the post office to have a coffee or something to eat.

The owner of the stall, Ibu Agus, was assisted by her daughter who had a younger brother who had not yet been circumcised. At first I would just have breakfast, but then as time went by I would go there every day to have lunch and dinner. Agus, the uncircumcised son, was always very happy when I went there. Usually if I had small change I would give it to him. One day all of a sudden he showed me a money box laden with coins. It gave me a real shock to see a young child who had been left behind by the death of his father. Juli, Agus's older sister, was a young woman who was devoted to her mother. Nearly every day she worked in the small food stall, except when she was washing the clothes in the house, spreading them out in the sun to dry, and sweeping up.

"Where do you work, sir?" Juli asked me one day. "You're very busy, always sending boxes of stuff through the post office."

"I work at home," I answered.

"Where's your office?" asked Juli.

"My office is as small as a box, a post box!"

Juli laughed. "So if you want to get into your office you have to turn into an ant!"

"Ah, maybe that's right, Juli," I said.

"But don't underestimate that," she said. "Ants set a good example to human beings, working together cooperatively, not getting angry, blood pressure going up like...."

"You're a fine one to talk!" said her mother.

"Oh, do you have high blood pressure?" I asked.

"No, my mother does. She's of noble Javanese stock, but now she works in a tiny lowly food stall like this," said Juli.

"It doesn't matter that it's just a box, the important thing is that it makes me a small amount of profit so that I can develop this box into a bigger building than my little post box. That's my food stall. I only make a little money, but luckily I'm just an ant so I don't eat much," I said. "Little people like us must start with a box."

"You can't be evicted from a post box, but if I don't pay the rent on this food stall they're threatening to evict us," said her mother. "People say that itinerant street traders with their food carts will be driven out and relocated, but in reality they just take their stuff away and pile it up in the yard of the mayor's office."

One morning when I arrived at the post office I saw that something was amiss at Ibu Agus's food stall. Two burly men were loading plates, pans, rice steamers, and so forth onto a pickup. When I asked, it appeared that Ibu Agus owed money to a loan shark. Ibu Agus was just sitting quietly staring in front of her, her face very red. Her blood pressure was high again. Juli could not do much, just be on hand to ensure her mother didn't burst a blood vessel as she feared. She could burst a nerve in her eye or her brain.

Although it was really none of my business, I felt compelled to ask, "How much do you owe them?"

"Only three hundred thousand, that man should have a heart," said Juli. "Besides which we had an agreement with him that we would pay him a thousand every day. Then suddenly he's asking us to pay back the whole amount because his house got flooded. Where are we supposed to find the money…"

"Actually we did have it, but yesterday we had to pay the doctor and the blood pressure tablets," said Ibu Agus.

I was no longer rational. I suddenly called out to the men, "Hey guys, put those things back in the shop. I'll pay what Ibu Agus owes," and with that I took three hundred thousand rupiah out of my wallet.

"Hmm, only three hundred, what about the interest? Our money's been sunk into this food stall for the last three years. Make it five hundred…"

"No."

"Why not?"

"Because I don't have any more money left. I only have three hundred."

"OK then, give us the money."

"Sure, but give back the lady's things first," I said.

A little while after the debt-collectors left, Agus came home from school. The little boy who had just started junior high school was surprised at what he found, and especially that there was nothing to eat. I told him to go and buy packets of rice for four people, and then set about helping to tidy up the food stall so that it did not look as if a bomb had hit it.

Ever since then, Juli would come to my rented room, to bring me food, to clean whatever needed cleaning, to wash my clothes, and to help me pack up the fans made of sandalwood and agarwood and to cut the agarwood into strips. Then after it was all packed neatly in cardboard boxes, she would write the name of the sender and the recipient and then would take them to the post office. She would also always open the post office box to retrieve the letters from my daughter. Juli had already become like my assistant. Even though she had gone only as far as junior high school, her handwriting was good and she was very smart at mental arithmetic.

After six months, disaster struck. Juli, who had no father, suddenly found a father in me and simultaneously fell in love with me. That filled me with a lot of conflicting emotions. I was fifty-five years old and Juli was only twenty. No, impossible. Poor Juli. But Juli dug her heels in and insisted that she wanted to be my wife. For me, this was no normal love, this was a bit like one of my sandalwood or agarwood fans which attracted money through their fragrance. If I didn't have money, no young girl would want me. Ah, the sandalwood fans, the agarwood fans, had rejuvenated this old man who already smelt of the soil. It was not proper for Juli to marry this mummified old pharaoh from Jakarta! Juli hugged me, pressing herself against my chest and said, "I will be there for you, even when you are so old that you need to use a stick. You will get your life back, you will rediscover your youth through our children."

I felt weak and dropped down onto the bed.

All of a sudden there was a knock on the door. As the door was not locked, she barged into the room. Her eyes were red. Maybe her blood pressure was high again. Her face was made up and she looked pretty, but because her lips were red with lipstick I felt as if a tiger had just come in.

"Juli is not a proper wife for you", she said. "But I am," she added, then went up to Juli and slapped her.

Juli ran out, and I went straight into the bathroom at the back and hid there for almost an hour. When I went back into my room, Ibu Agus had gone. Thank goodness.

After that I did not go back to Ibu Agus's food stall. I cancelled the subscription on my post box and transferred to a different post office.

About three months later, Juli came to my room, and sat feeding a baby with a bottle of milk. I was astonished. I hoped she had not come to extort money from me. Heaven forbid she would go to the police and report that this baby was my child, the child of a sandalwood fan trader.

"I'm living with a minivan driver," said Juli.

"And you've had a child already?" I asked.

"No. His wife ran away and gave her baby to me. I just took it. After all, what else could I do? My mother has high blood pressure. At least now I have a husband," said Juli, rocking the baby.

I said nothing. My eyes were wet.

A year later, I was riding my bicycle when I saw Ibu Agus dragging a half-full sack along the road. I stopped. She clearly no longer knew me, which was a shock. When I looked in her sack, I saw it was just filled with old water bottles and newspapers. Ibu Agus had become a scavenger. And Jakarta only gave her rubbish.

"Where's Juli these days?" I asked

"Juli died," she said.

"Where's Agus?" I questioned her again.

"At the crossroads, selling bottles of water," she answered.

"Where are you living, Ibu?"

"On people's verandas. There're lots of them, you just have to sleep there."

I was shocked.

"Who are you, sir?"

"I'm a sandalwood fan trader."

"Oh, help me, help me. Come on, give me a ride!"

After throwing away her sack of refuse, I took her on my bicycle to my room. I told her to take a bath and bought her some food.

The next day I took her to the mental hospital and then had her admitted to an old people's home.

The Thatched House
with a Stone Wall

Finally I returned to my former home, a thatched house with a stone wall around it. It was about fifty kilometers east of Kupang. Getting back to my old home was not easy, considering that all my children were living in Jakarta, had got jobs there, and were married with children. Their mother, who is not from the same part of the country as me, always threatened that if I went home to my village in Timor, she would go home to her family in the interior of Kalimantan, to the long house where she used to live on the edge of the forest beside the river.

Just imagine, she would have to take a boat to Pontianak and from Pontianak take a wooden boat, which they called a *badung*, and then proceed by motorboat as far as her village. Her village is twenty or thirty kilometers from Putussibau, so when my wife and her children went back home there, there was no communication between us. What made our children even sadder was that their mother came from a small Dayak tribe which still followed the tradition of putting their dead on a bamboo rack in the forest. At that time I had been head of the forestry office in Putussibau. On hearing the story that there was a corpse on a bamboo rack in the middle of the forest, one of my close assistants and I went to have a look. There I met a Dayak girl with smooth golden skin. Unusually, her ears had not been stretched and there were no tattoos on her body. In fact she was one of the few girls who had received an education and had already completed training as a midwife. As a daughter who was powerless to change their tradition, she could only witness her father's corpse placed on a rack in the middle of the forest. (There they did not bury their dead).

In the end I took her with me as my wife when I was transferred to Jakarta. We had six children. Indeed, a lot. Apart from the fact that in those days there was no contraception, we intentionally multiplied to prevent two minority tribes, the Dayak and the Timorese, from becoming extinct. I often joked with my children that maybe in fifty years' time, the arrogance of the majority ethnic group would disappear or at least diminish in the face of our children's efforts to increase the numbers of the minority Dayak and Timorese races.

Although there were many of them, we worked hard to give all our children an education and eventually they all graduated from university. But they were not obsessive about diplomas. Rather they were researchers who were faithful to truth and justice, if not yet of the stature of national thinkers.

When one of our children who had got a degree in forestry was posted to work near his mother's home area, she went home to her village. Strange as it was, she wanted to die there in the middle of the peaceful forest, not in the city jungle. But to travel such a long distance was not to be sneezed at, as things were not like they are now under the New Order. The New Order government has succeeded in reducing the distances between the different provinces. Now there are ships and planes. The main roads have been extended far into the interior. And because of that, it is easy for me now to get to my wife's village by plane and overland transport. Now we can use modern channels of communication like the telephone, telegrams, fax, and even internet. Actually I would quite like to live in my wife's home area, but the children do not agree. They say that I am still quite strong, so I am still able to help consolidate a future for our grandchildren. If we care about the future generations of our family, apart from education they should have geo-political strength all around this vast country of ours. As two of our children are economists, they helped us to set up a company through which we have established an agro-industry business. In West Kalimantan we grow oranges and coconut palms, and in Timor we have started rearing pigs and are cultivating five hectares of land.

So that was how it was, and finally I returned to my old home with the thatched house surrounded by a stone wall. But my five hectares of land were actually further inland, as my relatives were living in the house. Because I was so busy, I was rarely at that house, and besides I had already built a new house which was quite big but also thatched with straw with a stone wall around it. Outside the yard of my house, my land spread out in front of me. In the dry season I had cleared this land. Although the land was quite stony, it was still quite fertile and good for cultivating corn, mung beans, soy beans, bananas, papaya, coconuts, and in the spaces where there was more soil and fewer stones, I planted cassava which grew plentifully and very large. In fact the cassava that grows all around Timor is always very tender and tasty. I also planted pumpkins and small tomatoes.

Meanwhile I busied myself building an enclosure for local pigs and another for free-range chickens. My two children who graduated in economics came to have a look at the project. They built a shed with a roof made of palm fronds and a gate, for storing our produce from the land, and a few pens for the pigs and the chickens that would lay eggs. Quite unexpectedly, when my two children went around the island they saw much tamarind growing wild on the trees without anything being done to cultivate it. So they built another shed to store the produce gathered from the forest, particularly tamarind. Once it was ripe, they would study the market for tamarind in Java. Maybe they could set up a factory to produce canned or bottled drinks from this fruit, which was very high in vitamins.

As soon as the cassava began to take root, I started with one hundred pigs and five hundred free-range chickens. The enclosure for the pigs was not difficult to make. By arranging stones to make a wall around the enclosure, I could simply leave the animals to roam freely. If they were too hot, they just went into the shed. What to feed them was also not difficult, as the cassava roots that had just been pulled out of the earth could be thrown to them over the stone wall, and they gobbled them up with great enjoyment. They ate anything—banana stems, sweet potato leaves, and a sort of spinach from Manggarai called *bendes*. Once a week I asked my maid to cook soya beans mixed with corn and vegetables to feed to the pigs. They had all their food in the area below the pens, which was very fertile because in the rainy season the manure from the pens ran down onto the vegetable garden.

In the meantime, nearly all my children had visited to have a look at what I was doing, and I myself had flown to Jakarta a few times and then on to West Kalimantan to see my wife and to have a look at the oranges and coconuts. Not bad. Our agro-business grew substantially, and that made us all happy.

The only problem in all this was that my wife did not want to come to Timor, saying that she preferred me to fly to West Kalimantan. It looked like she preferred living near the forest rather than becoming a savannah dweller. She herself told her children that she preferred staying in their homes to look after her grandchildren. But I suspected that it was only her grandchildren who lived in her home village that got their grandmother's affection. Those who lived in Jakarta never got to see her, unless they went looking for her in the forests of Kalimantan.

Fortunately I was so busy organizing my planting and my animals that I never had a chance to feel lonely. And anyway I was good at keeping in touch by phone and mail, especially with deliveries of *dendeng* [smoked dried meat] almost every week. Besides that, an older woman who was a priest would often visit me with her children and grandchildren. She too had six children and a dozen grandchildren. Just imagine how they would come to that house thatched in straw with its wall made of stone sitting in the middle of an expansive piece of land which was also surrounded by a coral wall from my beloved island. They already felt completely at home in my house and garden.

The difference, though, was that this elderly woman had been a widow for many years. And the most important difference was that she did not have any children of her own, just the children of her relatives whom she had raised. They were all her nephews and nieces. This elderly woman was still an energetic preacher and taught in various schools. But people began to talk, asking why she had become so close to me, treating my house as if it were her own?

Forty years ago this elderly woman had once been a pretty young girl. Her eyes shone so beautifully and her eyelashes were so long that when I looked into her eyes it was as if I were seeing stars whose light shed a magnetic force, a piece of celestial beauty which had graced this Timorese savannah. Her skin was an attractive dark color and very soft, and I suspected from the first moment that it would not wrinkle like white or yellow skin. Indeed this elderly woman still looked young.

One evening, as I sat in front of my house chewing betel, I saw a woman come in through my garden gate and walk straight towards my house, right up to the veranda of my thatched house surrounded by a stone wall in the middle of the fields on the savannah. We looked at one another. Suddenly I saw the face of a pretty young girl with dark skin and long eyelashes. This was the girl who had once betrayed me. I chased away the feeling of resentment in my soul, for after all it was an elderly woman with a friendly air who was standing in front of me. I quickly forgot everything. I stood up and hugged and kissed her. Then she told me that she had just returned from the neighboring village where she had been conducting a religious service for the householders. Oh, that day I asked my helper to prepare a party. Before lunch we exchanged information on what we had both been doing. Before she left, I went into my bedroom and retrieved the engagement ring I had given her and which she had returned to me in a certain church after she broke off our engagement. Back then I truly felt I had been struck by lightning. I made an oath. I wrote my oath on a piece of paper then I cut my finger with a knife and placed a seal of blood on that letter.

"You're giving me back my ring? Where's that oath sealed with your blood?"

I ran back into my bedroom and fetched the oath to show her. She took it, lit a match, and burned it.

She sighed with relief. So did I.

"Come on, boy," I called to my helper. "Serve us our meal quickly to celebrate the reconciliation we'll now enjoy in our old age."

That afternoon I took her in my pickup to meet my children and grandchildren.

I told all this to my children in Jakarta, and unfortunately the news reached my wife in the middle of the forest in Kalimantan.

Suddenly my wife appeared. I was shocked. She had changed. She wanted to live in Timor and in fact now she lives with me in that thatched house surrounded by a stone wall enveloping us in a love that has no equal in our old age. But what really makes me shake my head is that my wife has changed her profession from being an old woman taking care of her grandchildren as she watched her husband work, to a woman who is always busy with something. Not busy looking after her old man, but busy taking care of the sick, visiting them and praying with them, leading church services and later on giving sermons in the church if the priest was not able to. As a result our spending has increased, as she always sets aside money to give to orphanages, old people's homes and such things.

What did my children say about this sudden change in their mother in her old age?

"As if pursued, you went as far as the South Pole in search of the love that was returned to you with that ring in the old church," said one of my children as we gathered around the dining table. "You even climbed to the Himalayas to cultivate the fields there trying to recapture your first love. Still as if pursued...!"

"It took jealousy to bring the forest of Kalimantan together with the savannah of Timor...!" said another.

"If a young girl is jealous, she drinks poison. If a young man is jealous he causes a revolution, but if an old woman is jealous she preaches through a loudspeaker..." said a third.

In that thatched house with the stone wall surrounded by the fields on the savannah, the dining table rocked with their laughter.

Pond of Gold

The old man sat on his own on the rock under the *jambu* rose-apple tree beside his pond of beloved fish in front of his house. The lamp in the middle of the pond cast a bright light. The afternoon rain had been long and plentiful, but it had made the night sky clear. The old man got up from where he was sitting and went into the house to fetch the rocking chair, then sat down in it and leaned back, making the chair rock back and forth.

First a couple of white ants that were flying around near the light fell into the water and the fish quickly swallowed them up. Then before long the lamp was surrounded by a cloud of flying ants, and the fish in the pond had a feast. "Life is all about being a victim!" he said.

His large house was in complete darkness, so the ants flew towards the lamp in the big pool. When his son and daughter-in-law with his only granddaughter came on holiday, he and his other son—who had been paralyzed since he was a small child and was now thirty—watched over the house from the pavilion on the side. When his wife died, he and that son lived in the pavilion and he handed over the big house to his married son.

Fortunately the pavilion they occupied had its own kitchen, bathroom, and toilet, freeing them from the need to engage in cold war. Then they were quietly both ignored. To start with, the maid did not sweep and mop their pavilion on a daily basis. Then left-overs of coffee, tea, and food from the big house were still set aside for the old man and his handicapped son, but everything was mixed with galangal, a spice which the old man hated the taste and smell of most of all. When he discussed this with his daughter-in-law, she just kept quiet and nothing changed in the way the food was prepared. Once when the old man came within a meter of the table, the smell of galangal was enough to send him running. He was forced to cook for himself.

Not long afterwards, the back door of the pavilion which connected it to the big house was closed. The reason given for this was that his daughter-in-law had to live at her mother's house, because it was near the hospital. In fact, even before they had got married, his daughter-in-law had suffered from heart and liver complaints and that's what made the old man angry with his son. He was especially disappointed that he had married an uneducated woman while his son himself had fought hard to get his master's degree and was now working as a police superintendent. When his son went off and got married in secret, the old man's whole body felt like collapsing. He staggered to the house of his son's first girlfriend and tearfully asked this girl, who was already working as a doctor at a private hospital, why the two of them had broken up. This girl, a clever, sweet doctor, just shrugged her shoulders, "I can show you the letter he sent me asking for us to break it off. You can read it for yourself."

"No need, it'll just make me feel even sadder," said the old man.

"The reason he gave for wanting to break up with me was just a pretense. I know exactly what the real reason was. To be honest, it was that my father once went to prison accused of smuggling morphine. But my father was framed by a drug syndicate. Somehow one day government officials turned up to search our shop and they found a packet of morphine hidden away in a corner. Heaven knows who put it there," said the pretty young doctor. "The consequence was that I lost my sweetheart," she said shedding tears.

"Oh my God, and my son married a woman who had once been illegally sent overseas as a foreign worker. Her father was a gambler, so he sold his daughter to a dealer in overseas workers. When my son got undercover work as a drug trader overseas, he met this woman in a bar and then somehow this woman came back to Indonesia and they got married without my approval. That was how it was. Why did my fate turn out like this?" said the old man, who was so unsteady on his feet that the pretty young doctor had to help him to a hospital bench.

After taking some medicine the old man was himself again. "Sorry, but I'm just confused about how to face my old age. I haven't any savings in the bank so I am obliged to cook for my handicapped son. It makes me sad. How can it be that they have holidays and go on trips all over the place, but they never take their handicapped brother with them? Luckily I've hired a swimming teacher, so the one diversion that my son has is swimming. But after building such a big house my savings are quite depleted. I saved up that money when I was captain of a big cruise ship. I have no one else in this world. And when I'm not around, what will happen to my handicapped son? Please see that he's put in a home for handicapped people."

"That's not a problem," said the pretty young doctor.

"So now I feel better. It's like this. I still have forty kilograms of pure gold in savings. I got all that when I was captain of the cruise ship which sailed around the world. I'll give it all to you so that you can look after my handicapped son."

"But also to cover the costs of your other son, the superintendent," said the pretty young doctor.

"What do you mean?" asked the old man.

"Your daughter-in-law has a liver disease. If your son does not use a condom, he'll also catch this disease. You'll use up your savings caring for both your sons," said his son's former girlfriend.

"Goodness. Why is everything such a mess? Can I make things better with this gold?" asked the old man.

"Let's hope so," said the pretty young doctor.

And so he handed over his savings, the forty kilograms of gold, to the pretty young doctor who used to be his son's girlfriend. From that time, on a courier organized by the pretty young doctor delivered all their daily needs, from shopping money to medicine.

That night he was sitting back peacefully. His soul was at peace, rocking back and forth in his chair beside the pond. The ants had gone and the pond was still, for the fish had eaten their fill and were no longer leaping.

All of a sudden two men jumped down from the high fence. They were both wearing masks.

"If you value your life, don't speak or shout out!" said one of them, and one taped his mouth shut while the other tied his hands and feet. They carried the old man to the pavilion and dumped him on the floor.

Then they threatened the handicapped son, who used two walking sticks. They taped his mouth shut and tied him up.

"Where's the gold?" asked one of them.

With his chin and his eyes the old man pointed towards the big house. Using a duplicate key, they opened the door and one of them went into the house. The other one guarded the old man and his son. Soon the man who had gone into the house came out again and shook his head.

"Un-tape his mouth so he can answer," said one of them.

They tore the tape off his mouth. The old man grimaced with pain but did not cry out.

"Where's the gold?"

"My son's already taken it," said the old man.

"That's a lie!" said one of the men, slapping him.

Because of his advanced age, he fainted immediately.

They turned off the pond light, then carried their two victims to the pond and threw them into the water.

Although the pond was deep and as large as a volley-ball court, the handicapped son managed to maneuver his body to the side and rubbed his mouth against the bank so that he was able to get the tape off. He then cried out so that the neighbors would hear him.

The old man was no longer alive when they fished him out of the pond. The police immediately called the son who was currently on holiday. A simple burial was arranged quickly while the police made a serious search of the house. As nothing was missing, it was all a bit of a riddle—but the mystery was solved straight away when the pretty young doctor came up with the information that the burglar had known that forty kilograms of gold had been stored in that house.

The police immediately concluded that this was an inside job. And the insiders were the eldest son himself with his wife behind the whole thing, and the two robbers were her relations.

An Aria to Travel

I finally reached Honolulu. After spending some time there, I got the feeling that there was nothing special about this place. It was just a big city which did not share many of the features of big cities in Indonesia. I roamed around here and there looking for Hawaiian girls, who they say are heavenly creatures descended to that tranquil sea, but it seemed that there were hardly any real Hawaiian girls. In a supermarket I met one girl with long dark hair and chocolate-colored skin. I was convinced that she was an original Hawaiian girl, but it turned out she was a mixture of Filipino and Japanese. Then when I saw a girl who looked as if she came from Papua, I thought she must be a real Hawaiian girl, but I was wrong again. That girl had curly hair like our Indonesian poet, Darmanto YT, and skin that was a little darker than that of our poet, but no, she was not Hawaiian either. She was a Negro girl whose mother had been from a white family.

As I wandered around Honolulu city I began to miss the cities of Indonesia because, whether during the day or at night, there was nothing that resembled our *kaki lima* sidewalk food stalls like back home. I missed sitting at a roadside food stall under the night sky, getting wet in the rain and sheltering under the makeshift tarpaulin, chatting to the girls serving me from Solo, Bogor, Sukabumi, Indramayu, and Cirebon. I missed talking about this and that till daybreak, like I was used to doing in my own country, then sleeping till eleven, then getting up, having something to eat and drink, then working for a while, then having lunch, then having a siesta, then waking up at half past three, getting up, bathing. And then after dinner I would go out again and roam around under the night sky, immersing myself in my beloved Indonesian underdogs, listening to them laughing and talking about nothing in particular, diving into the sad laments of the pretty *pesinden* singers from the north of West Java.

A few days in Honolulu made me really miss all that I have described above. But I was not going to go back to my homeland just like that. From Honolulu I had to continue my journey to Los Angeles. So, with my little bag I left the luxury hotel I was staying in and headed to the airport.

While I was waiting, all at once a Filipina girl sat down beside me. She spoke to me in Tagalog. I smiled at her, shook my head, and told her in English that I was not Filipino but Indonesian.

She asked me in English where I was going. Of course I told her that I was going to Los Angeles. On hearing that, she asked me if I would mind accompanying her on the journey. I was only too happy to have a travelling companion who was a pretty Filipina girl.

"Is it your first time to America?" I asked her in English.

"No, I've been twice before," she said.

"In that case you must help me so I don't get lost on the journey. It's my first time to the United States."

"But you won't get lost, as you can speak English," she said.

"Who knows. Do you work in America?" I asked.

"No, I've been studying in America for a long time, then I went back to the Philippines to do a bit of research and now I'm coming back to do my PhD," she said. "And you? Are you going to study in America?"

I smiled. "I'm a poet, who has been invited to read his poems," I said.

"I really like poetry!" she said.

"Did you graduate in languages?"

"No, I'm an anthropologist," she said.

"You should come to Indonesia. Indonesia is a researcher's paradise."

"Yes, I have family from Indonesia. I mean my sister-in-law is Indonesian. I'll introduce you to them if you'd like. My big brother married an Indonesian woman who's now living in Los Angeles. Oh, they're a big family. My sister-in-law has a lot of brothers and sisters. Her parents passed away in America two years ago, but their children are never lonely. They maintain an international family through marriage," said the Filipina.

"By the way, what's your name?" I asked.

"Estrella," she said.

"My name's Suharto," I said.

"Ah, so you're the President of Indonesia?" she said, laughing.

"Ah," I replied also laughing. "In the Philippines there're lots of people called Jesus but they're not the savior of all mankind!"

We got closer and closer.

When we first got on the plane, we were sitting in separate seats but then we looked for empty seats so that we could sit together on the long journey from Hawaii to Los Angeles.

"Are you married?" asked Estrella.

"No," I answered. "And you?"

"Me neither," she answered.

"So in that case let's get married," I said.

"That's quick!" Estrella shrieked.

"Yes, what I most fear is solitude," I said.

"But I don't know you yet," said Estrella.

"When we get off the plane, we'll go straight to a psychiatrist." I said.

"What on earth for?"

"So you can find out all about my psyche and see if it's normal or a bit crazy," I said.

Estrella laughed and shrugged her shoulders. "The poet lives close to a world considered crazy. One of my relatives is like you. He talks completely without inhibitions and he writes poems and short stories. His wife and child really suffer, especially when he was arrested over one of his short stories."

"If that's the case, I horrify you. I'm sure you'll turn down my proposal," I said.

"Don't say that, darling," she said. "I've already told you that I love poetry, right?"

"But not the poet. I don't have anything to offer you, except all the beautiful islands of Indonesia that I've already captured in my poems. You need to come and do your research in Indonesia. I'm sure you'll not be disappointed in the food. I'll prepare mountains of fish and mountains of sago for a beautiful anthropologist like you," I said.

"I don't need all that," she said.

"What do you need?" I asked.

"What I need is a man who is really genuine," she answered.

"There're lots of genuine men in Indonesia," I said. "Did you ever hear about the American female graduate who married the chief of a tribe in Papua who still wear penis gourds? Now there's a genuine man for you!"

"No, no, that's not what I mean, you crazy Indonesian!" she said tugging on my arm.

The stewardess served dinner and we enjoyed it as we flew over the Pacific Ocean. After dinner, Estrella got sleepy. But before she went to sleep, she got out a magazine about Filipino culture and thrust it at me.

"Read a short story from this magazine. It was written by my cousin. I like his poetry, but I'm not so keen on his short stories. It's as if I'm looking at myself. But that is the face of so many Filipino women who lead a wretched life in this transitory world of ours. I hope that Indonesia does not have such women," she said. "But even if there are women like that in Indonesia, they probably still need a writer like my cousin who converts their story into fiction," said Estrella. Then she wrapped a blanket around herself and closed her eyes.

The title of this short story was "Hero." In essence this is what it was about.

It was a Saturday night. Mr. Alfonso, the director of a joint venture company, went out around the city with his driver. To start with they took the main road running alongside the beach, enjoying the cool night wind blowing in from the sea. Then they had dinner. They chose the nicest looking beachside restaurant, where they had the best food. For Mr. Alfonso was quite a philanthropist. He was also considered quite democratic, at least in the way he treated his loyal driver. Alfonso was also quite a philanthropist in the eyes of all the pretty girls who led a life of hardship. And that's how it was for Theresa.

"Once you've eaten, you go and pick Theresa up," said Mr. Alfonso to his driver.

"Right, sir!" said the driver jumping to attention like a soldier.

"Arnaldo!" said Mr. Alfonso.

"Yes, sir!" said the driver.

"Bring Theresa to Villa Gatella in Tanjung The Singha."

"Yes, sir!"

"Meanwhile phone Mercedes III to pick me up. If my son is using it, then just call Mercedes XI," said Mr. Alfonso.

"Yes, sir."

Soon after the driver had left, a Chinese girl turned up and sat down at Mr. Alfonso's table. She was a pretty girl and had been a friend of Mr. Alfonso's for some time. That night the Chinese girl, by some instinct, sensed that this man, who was the richest man in the Philippines, did not require her services. Because she understood this, she just sat quietly, serving Mr. Alfonso in whatever way she could, and this included doing his nails. And she was right, that night Mr. Alfonso did not require her services, even though she was one of the prettiest girls in the Philippines. She was of mixed blood. Her great-grandfather had been a pirate in the South China Sea. When he landed in the Philippines he had married an indigenous Malayan Filipina. And then later, when the Spanish arrived, their blood got mixed in with that of this Chinese girl's forebears. Imagine, how could she not be pretty and also smart? Yes, this Chinese girl was exceedingly pretty and very smart. She had been part of Mr. Alfonso's life for some time now and understood the intricacies of his joint venture business. She started off as a secretary, but after she had his child, she became very wealthy. She opened two hundred restaurants all around the Philippines and a real estate business, and she also owned a pleasure boat. But Mr. Alfonso never used that boat. What for? Better to leave it for the Chinese girl to enjoy with her boyfriend.

His driver, Arnaldo, was someone who knew how to show gratitude. Having already worked for Mr. Alfonso as his personal driver for fifteen years, he could easily have quit his job. But he was not stupid. As Mr. Alfonso's personal driver, whenever he went out, and especially on a Saturday night, he got paid for sitting around drinking without having to spend a cent. But it was not as if Arnaldo had not opened his own business with the capital he had got from Mr. Alfonso. As the richest driver in the country, he had already opened fifty luxury traditional massage parlors in various cities in the Philippines. He had learned a lot from his boss about investing in low-risk businesses. According to Mr. Alfonso, a country like the Philippines produced a lot of beautiful women who were living in poverty. That's the way it was. Arnaldo picked up low-class prostitutes from under bridges and railway carriages, scrubbed them with carbolic acid, gave them nice clothes, and trained them to be traditional masseuses. He put the women on display behind glass shop fronts while they waited for customers to come for their massages. He made a decent living out of it. His wife was happy and his children were able to get a good education.

While members of parliament criticized putting pretty women on display behind glass windows, if they closed down the massage parlors, what would happen to all these pretty Filipina women? Would they have to go back to living under a bridge or a railway carriage?

Not to mention Mr. Alfonso, who sold wood from the forests of the Philippines. He generated foreign exchange. He also imported big saws, tractors, and other heavy equipment from Japan and other industrial nations, as well as importing the very biggest cars. And nobody could criticize him. Or, if he was criticized, he could easily brush it off with some well-constructed argumentation and a bit of political pressure. And the fact that he had made his name as a brave fighter in the armed insurrection in the Southern Philippines strengthened his support. He had risen through the ranks from captain to major, to brigadier general, to lieutenant general, to major general, to full general. When he retired he dedicated himself to his beloved Philippines as a big businessman. For in fact Mr. Alfonso was a clever man, not just in the military field, but also in the area of international trade.

And let's not forget, he was an industrialist, and industrial progress in the Philippines could be attributed to the efforts of Mr. Alfonso. So it was only fitting that people should say that Mr. Alfonso was a businessman who understood the art of doing business. He was an artist in his own field. People said that as an artist he loved beauty, and because of that he was always in the vicinity of beautiful women. And Mr. Alfonso's wife knew this and understood. Mrs. Alfonso was an educated woman. She had come to understand how it was for Japanese businessmen surrounded by geishas; she read books about the harems of Arabia; she recognized how attractive and submissive Javanese women were; she read *Playboy*; she read poetry saying that French women made good wives, Chinese women made good cooks, and Japanese women were born to serve. She could not prevent her husband reading such stuff, but the important thing was that the business of this important national businessman ran smoothly.

That night the Chinese girl served him the most delicious Chinese food. After dinner the Mercedes XI arrived and his driver took Mr. Alfonso to his own luxury villa on the promontory.

This driver, who had been arranged by his trusted driver Arnaldo, sent a message to headquarters that Mr. Alfonso was now at the villa with Theresa. Because of the prevailing conditions, it was important to know where Alfonso was at all times. Recently Alfonso's family had been busy preparing for the huge wedding of Alfonso's daughter, in accordance with Filipino traditions so as to promote tourism. According to the driver, the daughter's wedding present from her father was a pleasure boat, and from her mother, a Mercedes and a cute little palace on a bare hillside with water pumped up from the river forty kilometers away. The cost of the wedding was calculated at around five million dollars! And all because of the love of a father for his daughter who was marrying the son of a black magic specialist. Really, he was an exemplary father.

And who was Theresa? Theresa was a girl who had worked as a servant at the Santa Ursula convent. She was a village girl who had not been able to get an education, as her parents were only poor farm workers who climbed coconut palms to get the coconuts. When her father fell out of a coconut palm and broke his leg, Theresa became a washerwoman in the convent for a very small wage. One day when her mother was sick with malaria and the wages of her brother were not enough to buy the medicine, Theresa applied to work in Arnaldo's traditional massage business. Arnaldo realized that this girl was still a virgin, so he hurried to report this to his boss, Mr. Alfonso. Now this virginal girl is on cloud nine, even if she has been soiled by money and the luxury of this villa. But what is to be done? That is the fate of a pretty young girl from the village.

In the early hours, at three in the morning, the whole of Villa Gatella Bragandha was in panic. They were phoning the hospital and the best doctors. An ambulance sped towards Tanjung The Singga with its red lights flashing. And what was all this about? Suddenly this sixteen-year-old girl realized that the heart of the tough old man of sixty-two had stopped. She called the servants and the police dogs, who surrounded the villa....

In the Heroes' Cemetery of the Philippines, the burial of a big national hero was taking place. All the high-ranking officials of the land were in attendance along with all the big businessmen and industrialists. And the common people were also there. But what happened then? Among the honor guard, there was one young soldier who looked a bit crazy. When they were ordered to fire their guns in homage, suddenly this young man started firing shots into the coffin. Who would not have panicked? And who was this crazy shooter who had infiltrated the ranks of the riflemen? It turns out it was Theresa's brother!

I woke up Estrella with a kiss. She sat up and looked at me. "Are we there?" she asked smiling.

"I've finished it," I said giving her back the magazine. "I'm also afraid of getting shot. Look how quickly I fell in love with you and proposed to you in the space of this short journey."

She smiled, moved closer to me, and put her head on my shoulder, then whispered, "I'm not just another Filipina girl, I'm Estrella, a grown-up woman who's very lonely," she said.

"Wed yourself to your science, not to this poor wretched poet," I said.

"Yes, I haven't married any poet yet. I have just met a poet who wanted to give me poetry and I gave him an aria to travel. Right?"

"Right!" I said.

We were like a couple of brown pigeons wrapped in a blanket in the belly of the jumbo jet. In front of us sat an English couple. The man said, "Kiss me, kiss me." And I repeated the same words to Estrella.

The Pearl Family

We were a family with the sea in our blood. Although our little island home was quite fertile and our land produced plentiful supplies of peanuts, corn, gourds, and rice, although coconuts, breadfruit, and mangoes flourished, still we depended on the sea. It was not that we could not raise livestock on our island, we could, but our island was small and we were surrounded by the vastness of the sea.

I am sure that when our forefathers first arrived on the island, they lived on seafood. They ate a lot of fish and a bit of sweet potato, bananas, and breadfruit. Then to satisfy their need for carbohydrates, they took the sap from the Palmyra palm and made sugar. They drank sugar and ate fish, shellfish, and vegetables which they found on the land as well as in the sea.

Indeed, we are surely descendants of the sea, not just because we eat seafood but also because of all the boats to be found on the beaches of our little island. That is proof that our ancestors came to this island by boat, and their descendants have continued the tradition of building boats and sailing from island to island in the waters of Indonesia and even crossing the ocean to discover the shores of Australia, Africa, and Asia.

But despite what has been passed down from our ancestors, not everyone became a child of the sea. Because our little island is prosperous. Some settled on the land, not caring for the waves and the seasonal winds that fiercely buffeted the sails of the boats, pulling them in all directions. Some made big houses out of large, solid pieces of wood, from the trunks of the giant trees that were hundreds of years old and had died of old age. The high quality of the wood of these tree trunks inspired the creation of a traditional style of architecture that was undeniably beautiful, undeniably strong, combining as it did symbolic meaning and a sense of the practical. Our traditional houses were built for the gods but also to protect those living in them from the fierce winds blowing in from far lands across the ocean. The surrounding high wall was made of stones or pieces of coral. To start with my ancestors' home was a fortress. Up to the present day we still have one of those old traditional houses surrounded by a stone wall. Around that fortress other houses grew up as our ancestors' family grew. When the tide went out, those living inside and outside the fortress would go down to the sea to look for food, keen to eat fish, shellfish, and seaweed, bored with eating chicken, goat, mutton, buffalo, and such like.

Civilization arrived. Chinese traders landed on our shores. Their junks brought porcelain and silk, coins, beads, and swords, and all sorts of rifles and other weapons. All this was exchanged for sandalwood, mung beans, and the skins of crocodiles and snakes. Then came the Portuguese and the Dutch. They brought schools and teachers who, to begin with, were paid in mung beans, rice and honey. Later when a currency had been established, they were paid a proper salary.

As far as I remember, the older people say that the first school was set up on my little island around the year 1700. That means that this island has had schools for nearly three hundred years.

Maybe it was this schooling that gradually made it possible for the islanders to become sailors, then for the settlers of these fortress-like houses who ploughed the fields and raised livestock and planted coconut trees and such things to go out from the island. Some left their homeland as seafarers, some worked in private companies and with the colonial government, some became soldiers and traders.

Among those who left the island was my father. He worked in the office of the colonial government on another larger island. So I grew up as the son of a government official rather than that of a sailor or a farmer.

I have a vivid memory of how I began to become aware of this world when a parcel arrived one day from the post office. When I opened it, my father cried, "Wow, shoes, wow, a gramophone, wow, what else is there?" My mother carried on unpacking the parcel. "Oh, a little bottle of pearls." The bottle was made of porcelain and was opaque.

I tried on the shoes. I felt as if I was standing on two small canoes, because the shoes were far too big for a child like me. I walked round the living room, and into the kitchen and the bedroom wearing those shoes that had arrived in the post.

For the very first time I heard the sound of singing and musical instruments emitting from a box which had a big loudspeaker attached to it. This gramophone had a picture of a dog on it so, to this day, I refer to it as the dog snout gramophone. Every day, as soon as he came home from the office, my father would put on the gramophone, especially when he was having lunch. Also when he was reading at night before he went to sleep.

The thing that most impressed me was the little bottle of pearls. My father took some cotton and a handful of raw rice grains. According to my father, the rice grains would be eaten by the pearls so that they would gradually get bigger. In the imagination of a small child like me, there had to be a miraculous creature hiding inside the pearls which emerged at night to eat the rice grains.

Father really loved those shoes, the gramophone, and the bottle of pearls. He never wore the shoes but asked Mother to put them away in the cupboard.

Those three strange objects had been sent by his younger brother. Ages ago his younger brother had left home and gone far away to Australia. Father said that he was working in a town called Broome on the west coast of Australia in a pearl diving company. He earned quite a good salary, which meant that he could send my father those shoes, the gramophone, and the pearls.

I still remember, not long after having received that package from Broome, my father was transferred to a town which was a busy port. Commercial ships and all sorts of different boats came and went, among them steamers and a sailing boat which people called a schooner. The owner was an Englishman, but it turned out that his wife was related to us. They had come from Teluk Mutiara [Pearl Bay], where there were a lot of pearls, and this schooner was especially for pearl divers.

The owner of this schooner whose wife was related to us was quite fortunate. He had four children, two boys and two girls. Since they were now of school age, they had come to live in our port town. Once a month, the father would come to see his wife and the children. As an only child, I was happy to have gained new playmates. I was the same age as the second child. The first child was a boy who was famous for his prowess at swimming. From him I received swimming lessons so that, although I was still small and had not yet started school, I was already able to swim and dive. We played on the beach and swam in the sea almost every day. Like little birds flying in the sky, we never got tired of the water, swimming for hours until dusk was upon us.

When the schooner arrived from Teluk Mutiara, we would swim out to the boat. We would take off our shorts and shirts and would hold them up in the air with one arm to keep them dry while we swam with the other arm and both legs. But it was not just the schooner that made us swim so skillfully out to sea and with so much enthusiasm. We were even more motivated if commercial ships or steamers arrived to unload and load their goods. As our port did not have a quay where the ships could dock, all the ships and boats were obliged to moor some way out to sea, drop their anchors, and spend several days there. So nearly every day we would swim out to the ships. We would swim around the ships and ask the passengers to throw us coins. We would try and catch the coins either with our mouth or our hands or dive down and fetch them.

From an early age I could already swim for hours chasing the coins which people threw to us. If we felt tired, we would climb up onto the ship and buy food and drink from the little store on board.

One day the ship's captain called us and gave us delicious food and drink. Also cakes and expensive bottles of soft drinks. And all for free. All because of those mixed-blood little girls. Maybe they had got fed up because they had to wait too long on the beach. They tried to swim out to the ship. They actually managed to swim as far as the ship and then dangled on the ropes, shouting for their big brothers. The older brother was angry and shooed them away, but they swam towards the ladder, jumped up, and climbed up the ladder stark naked. They were very happy that they had been able to follow us from the beach. On seeing that these two mixed-blood girls had been brave enough to swim far out from the beach to the ship, the captain called them and picked them both up in his arms. He gave them clothes and tasty food and drinks.

Before long, the girls would swim with us boys on the beach and even out as far as the ships. Strange. We never worried about the sharks which might attack children swimming near the commercial ships moored there. Once, it is true, there was a disaster out at sea, but not because of sharks. One day a child was swimming and dived underneath a motorboat which connected the ship and the shore, pulling barges and picking up passengers. Suddenly the child's body got caught in the motorboat's propeller and he was killed. After that incident our parents forbade us to swim out to the ships and to play around them, but we did not stay out of the sea for long. Once our parents calmed down again, we went back to our swimming.

When I was in the second year of elementary school, I saw that the wife of the owner of that schooner had given my mother a small bottle of pearls. Mother then took a bigger bottle to keep them in and to "cultivate" those pearls by feeding them raw rice. And then one day my father suddenly turned up with five or six white spheres that resembled pearls. Father said that those balls were coconut pearls. Someone had found them inside a coconut and Father had bought them straight away.

By chance, in that port town there was a married couple who were also related to my mother, who were goldsmiths. Mother had a pearl necklace made, plus a ring and also a pair of earrings. My mother was a pretty woman and was all the more attractive when she was wearing traditional dress (woven ikat cloth) together with pearl and gold jewelry.

My mother was probably the happiest woman on this earth. She had already been given two small bottles of pearls by her in-laws and family. And she had not had to pay a cent for them. She would repay that kindness in some form or another, even if not directly to those who had given her the pearls. My mother always had an open house for the pearl divers. She gave them food, or medicine if they were suffering from malaria or flu. Or if one of them had been injured, my mother would treat them. My mother happened to know something about how to heal those who were suffering from minor ailments or even something more serious like malaria. For in fact, when my mother was younger, she had trained as a nurse and had also worked in a hospital before my father had asked for her hand in marriage.

Among the divers there were some who had lost their hearing, so when they reached our home, they made a lot of noise. Maybe not for them, but for us it was a real commotion. Their voices were very loud, and when we talked to them we had to talk loudly too. There was one man who was a drunk, which did not make my mother happy, but what could she do? The good thing was that if that diver had drunk a lot, the worst that could happen was that he would sing very loudly and then fall asleep.

One day, when our family members who were goldsmiths had gone to the house of the wife of the schooner owner to make a gold necklace and a pearl pendant, that drunken diver turned up and somehow took a slug of liquor, hurled it down his throat, then, oh, oh, oh, he was confused for a moment because the liquor burned his mouth and throat. Then he fell to the ground, and just like that was suddenly dead. I and the mixed-blood children of the Englishman saw him collapse before our eyes.

What happened that day bemused me. I was still small, but I was already beginning to ask myself why people valued these small spheres called pearls so highly. Why did people wear themselves out on that schooner to get those little round balls, and why did they use divers wearing all kinds of strange clothing to dive down to the bottom of the sea, even if it meant they lost their hearing? Why!

That night I took the bottle of pearls out of the cupboard and looked at it closely. Mother saw me and put it back in the cupboard. I was curious. I waited for the right opportunity. One day when my mother and father had gone to the burial of one of the divers who had had an accident on the bottom of the sea, I took out the bottle of pearls. I really wanted to see the little creature that was somehow able to come out and look for the food provided for it and gobble it up. It was amazing that there was a little animal inside the pearl which ate only rice grains.

I chose the largest pearl. I took a hammer and a sheet of iron and smashed it. I looked inside it, but it was no use. I took another one, then a second, a third, a fourth, until I had smashed between ten and twenty pearls. All in vain. Then I imagined that it was as if these small animals were enchanted. Every molecule of this powder was an animal. How would it be if I put a spell on all these pearls, then put them away and a few days later looked at them to see what reaction there had been, if they had changed and such like? Maybe they would be better than the original pearls.

So I crushed all the contents of that bottle very finely. It was really cool. The pearls had become a powder, but not any old powder. This powder would assume strange forms. After the whole lot had been converted into powder—of course there were still some bits which were less fine—I put it all back into the bottle. I put the opaque porcelain bottle back where it had been before, in a small box in the cupboard where my mother kept her jewelry.

Strange. Mother never checked. Maybe it was because that was when the Japanese landed and we were too busy looking at what the troops were up to, Mother forgot to keep an eye on her property. Suddenly we heard that the Japanese had seized all my family's wealth, starting with the schooner and ending with them taking the life of the owner. The husband of that family was dragged away and killed. The wife and children had nothing left and came to my mother asking for help. Mother took the bottle out of the heavy old teak cupboard. Suddenly she screamed when she saw the powder, which looked just like ash.

A Family of Wanderers

Goodness me! It turned out that the fate of us four brothers and sisters was to wander the globe. Imagine, just recently I heard my youngest sibling talking away on a Dutch radio station about our family. It was in fact my youngest sister, Fien, a high school biology teacher in Holland, and her husband, a Dutchman with Papuan blood, heaven knows from where in Papua. Her husband was a clever man. Observing how clever he was, I often wondered if his mother was descended from coastal people. For let's compare him with our family, descended from coastal folk who lived in a house with a thatched roof with a coral-stone wall around it. And under the thatched roof there were bamboo platforms full of rice and fish which had been dried in the yard of our house. A vast yard, as vast as the one at the presidential palace in Bogor. There was so much salted fish around that our noses were used to its pungent smell, so much so that if someone came to our house smelling of perfume, I would embarrass my town-dwelling family members by vomiting, as I was allergic to the smell of perfume.

My brother-in-law's sense of smell was not like mine, but of course his ancestors had eaten a lot of fish and shellfish and there were a number of them who were real geniuses; but they were all erased from the list of the most learned people in the world, with the exception of my brother-in-law. This brother-in-law of mine, with his mix of Dutch and Papuan blood, was quite a famous professor of biology in Europe. He was a researcher who also took his responsibilities as a father very seriously and paid a lot of attention to the education of his two children, who were also highly intelligent. I was very proud of him. I only regret never being able to see him. I had not been able to see them since they got married in Indonesia. Actually my sister's family did have a holiday in Indonesia on one occasion, but once they got here, they decided they preferred the Badui, Balinese, Tengger and Dayak people. They spent only one night in my home and then flew off around this land of myriad islands of ours.

Listening to my sister's voice on the Dutch radio and even after her voice had vanished, I missed her. She was so near yet so far from us all, and especially from me. Oh God, why is it our fate as human beings to live like this? When we were small and lived together in the same house—that thatched house with the coral-stone walls and the aroma of fish—they were heavenly days. What I remember most vividly was my little sister's creativity. One time we were coming home from the fields at dusk. We had reached the small spring which gushed out from the coral rocks shaded by huge mango and jackfruit trees laden with fruit, so we could bathe before going home. As she was carrying spring water home on her shoulders (I was carrying firewood), she said to me, "So if life goes on like this, what will we become?"

"What?" I said, confused, not suspecting that this little girl, my kid sister, could suddenly come out with such reflections. At that time, she had stopped attending elementary school in the second year and I was in the third year. For the past year we had both helped my mother and our two older siblings to clear our corn, rice, and barley fields of weeds. We also grew millet, *turi* beans, and squash on our land. When it was the dry season, we planted our family's land with onions, tobacco, and cabbage.

My little sister who had had to drop out of school carried her water in a container made of palm leaves, saying nothing. Then suddenly she said, "I don't want to become like our brother and sister. They're quite happy to have left school after their third year and accept their destiny as uneducated farmers. I can't do that. I need to go back to school."

Now when I reflect on this, I am tempted to conclude that this idea, or interest, or desire was sent to my little sister by God. She received Divine inspiration to change her destiny and the destiny of us all as she sat by that pretty little spring shaded by mango and jackfruit trees. I could even imagine that in those trees there resided guardian angels of the spring, and it was they who whispered to her and gave my little sister the idea, the interest, and the desire to go back to school. I say it was her destiny and then the destiny of all four of us siblings, because, goodness knows how, my little sister persuaded our older brother and sister, and they went together to meet the teacher (without our mother or father knowing, as they were busy in the fields) and happily the teacher agreed to accept all four of us. We all went back to school.

So that was what happened. After we successfully completed university, I am sure that it was not just our ideas, our desires, and our passion as human beings with all our limitations which accounted for our accomplishments. It was not because we had lived in that thatched home with the coral-stone wall and the smell of fish either. For me, there was a Divine love which was concealed from us but which we felt clearly and was proven in the way we were all able to complete our education in our respective fields. Hard work and both spiritual and physical suffering were the steps towards the heights of a life of civilization and culture for us four brothers and sisters. But was it not God who created these steps?

Once my elder brother started school again, he was always top of his class until finally he was accepted into the College of Higher

Education for Philosophy and Theology in Ledalero. Unfortunately, as soon as he became a priest, he was transferred to our neighboring country, the Philippines, and then, who knows how it came about —most likely because the struggling of his soul saw the suffering of the downtrodden—suddenly we received the news that he had joined the communist guerrillas and gone into the jungle. We only got the news from the radio and television that our big brother had been shot dead by government forces. A real tragedy, he was such a clever man. Very strong-willed, his head full of radical, populist ideas and maybe a real sense of compassion for the little people—all this made him fall prey to a group of angry people set on revenge. But who knows. These are just my limited musings, the musings of a human being who takes a long-term view of life different from my older brother's. We are left with the eternal question as to why the world is full of paradoxes, why my elder brother, who had already chosen the path of love, got mixed up with a group who committed themselves to bloodshed. It makes me sad, it gives me a tremendous sense of loss, it makes me miss my controversial brother so much as the questions go round and round in my head, unanswered.

My big sister, the second-born in our family, ended up completing her studies in the Faculty of Economics. Once she had graduated, she set up her own business. She planted part of our family's land with cotton, indigo, and other plants used for making natural dyes. Then she opened a weaving business. She became very successful and sent her weaving to Australia. She opened a small shop in Darwin which made her a reasonably good living. Then suddenly an Australian businessman asked her to marry him. Now she flies back and forth from Darwin to Kupang to Rote, all those islands where we came from. Although her land is full of coral, it is good soil for planting cotton. She has also opened a number of guesthouses in our village, so that many of our relatives have got work in the business which she set up with her husband.

I am the only one living alone in Jakarta. Once I retire, I will go and live on my beloved little island, Rote, in a house with a thatched roof and a coral-stone wall, breathing in the smell of fish every day. That's my plan. I have been saving for years, and with part of these savings I bought a four-thousand-square-meter piece of land in Jakarta. For years, too, I have been saving from my salary as a mathematics lecturer at a state university so that I could build my own house. Fortunately when I was small, I had dropped out of school and worked in the fields from six o'clock in the morning until four o'clock in the afternoon, so my muscles are used to manual work. That means that alongside the workers that I hire to do the heavy work, I also do the lighter jobs.

That means the money I spend on the house is not too much. I am very thankful that I have given up smoking. It's strange. Since I was small, we have always cultivated tobacco. The money I would have spent on smoking I channel into the house. Yes, I have a beautiful house which is clean and modern, as it was designed by one of my colleagues who is a lecturer in architecture. When I sell this house, I will use the capital to reclaim the thatched house with the coral walls and the aroma of fish.

That is my big dream, but I will not achieve it completely. Nobody fulfils such big dreams absolutely. Human beings are born to wander, even if they end up settling in their village, or in a thatched house on the beach with a coral-stone wall and the aroma of fish. For me a human being's vessel for wandering the world is his age. Aging is identical with the process of weathering and corrosion, and we humans can only be truly human by using our abilities to stop the rot through photography, painting, literature, theatre, or dance. But I am not an artist. How can I stop this process of corrosion and create something which has some sort of artistic permanence? Perhaps I cannot aspire to this. I actually have a few artistic photos taken with my girlfriend, Maryam, as we hugged each other with our cheeks pressed close together, but what I miss is not what is in those photos. I want there to be something eternal that will be useful to humanity.

And for that reason, when I became a mathematics lecturer in a country which is prone to these sentiments, I wrote a number of books on mathematics for the less fortunate middle schools and universities, which the government procured through a presidential program to distribute to school and university libraries throughout the country. To prevent negative religious sentiments fostering intolerance and fanaticism, my book even went to libraries in mosques, churches, Hindu temples and Buddhist *vihara*. The amusing thing is that people look in a book of mathematics to find a code for gambling. But what really makes my heart tremble is seeing how such animalistic sentiments can gain political strength and through a mathematical process can be used to put people down and even kill people who are fellow citizens of this country and of the world.

What is truly horrifying is how logic is used to justify terrorism, either on the part of individuals or by groups or even countries. What is truly horrifying is how rational logic cannot be tamed by a logic determined by conscience. I am horrified. I am often horrified when I find my head completely dominated by masculine, logical, rational formulae, and I can only find balance if there is a woman in my life. But what can I do about this? There is an animal instinct in human beings. There are very rational human beings and human beings who are dominated by their feelings. Maryam has already left me with all sorts of dark feelings which are difficult to break through with mathematical logic. What can I do? And I say once again, what can I do? The important thing was that my wounded heart was not looking for revenge, triggering a response that would unfold with mathematical precision. No. I was still mysteriously guided by my conscience and driven by the love of the Almighty.

Apart from the fact that all this time I had been engaged in an intellectual struggle to find something new that would benefit the world and all mankind and make this nation proud.

For years I had been dreaming of discovering an innovation in the field of mathematics, for years I had been dreaming of marrying an entrepreneur who could find something new, and because of that I lost Maryam. I thought if I lived on my own without Maryam, my beloved girlfriend who left me, then at least I would be able to create something innovative in my career as a scientist, but it had all been to no avail. I do not believe this was because I am not capable of achieving this, but because of health issues. All at once I was taken by surprise by the realization that there was something wrong with my gall bladder. Luckily those inhuman stones could be dealt with from the outside, without the need to open up my belly, as had been the case with previous patients suffering from this complaint. It was all thanks to the latest innovation in the field of medicine. In my solitary wandering with all its threats and dangers, I was helped by a number of women working in the field of science and technology, the modern equivalent of guardian angels who prevented me from dying.

Every day I took care of myself. I watched my diet carefully. I shopped and cooked for myself. My diet consisted of certain fruits and vegetables and anything that would not be toxic for me. And so solitude and loneliness became part of my wandering existence. My two sisters often sent me letters and sometimes called me.

After spending holidays in Holland and Australia, my sisters suggested that I should use my next time off to visit our old village, which I had not been back to in a long time. It seems that our old home, with the thatched roof and the stone wall and the aroma of fish, was still there and was the home of our father's youngest brother. He was already very old but could still walk to the fields and the beach. That made me feel more enthusiastic and increased my passion for life.

It had been a long rambling journey which had been diverted from its original goal by my ill health, but now I felt I had found a new goal: to rediscover the house with the thatched roof, the coral-stone wall, and the aroma of fish. A new home within the old memories.

So my little sister flew from Holland to Jakarta. I met her at Soekarno-Hatta airport, and after she had spent one night in my home, we flew together to Kupang. Our older sister who lived in Australia was already waiting for us in Kupang. After overnighting in Kupang, the three of us flew to Rote and then rented a vehicle to take us to the house with the thatched roof, the wall of coral-stone, and the aroma of fish.

Sculpture

My name is Ngurah. I'm originally from Bali, from a village called Pelaga, famous for its vegetables, its sweet potato, and its tranquility. When I was still small I moved away from my beloved village to live at the foot of the mountain where the land was fertile, much more fertile than in my birthplace. I feel that I'm not going to talk very much here about my childhood. Suffice it to say that I have not been circumcised.

As was usual in these modern times, my parents made sure I had a good education. First I was sent to elementary school, then junior high school, then senior high school, and then I entered the Indonesian Academy of Fine Arts (ASRI) and became a sculptor. I'm a Balinese sculptor, but at the same time an Indonesian sculptor. No! Over and above being an Indonesian sculptor from Bali, I am a creator of sculpture who is proud of his profession. My works have already been circulated to all corners of my country and even the world, especially to America and Europe. And all because of the help I got from Windy, an American girl I met some five years ago.

Throughout those five years we kept in contact. The letters we wrote were strictly about business, the business of sculptures, batik, paintings, sandalwood fans and such like. We never spoke of love, because, even though we had been sweethearts for two weeks back then, what was the point in thinking about that now? Five years but a million miles away from each other had killed off any interest we might have had in getting married. She had already married and divorced, and I too had got married, and had four children, and then also had got divorced, and was now living on my own, roaming from village to village, town to town, making sculptures and paintings and selling them. I hardly ever went home, because the mother of my children had remarried. Oh my! I am one of God's creature destined to be lonely, and I believe I would have gone crazy if it had not been for my creative talents. I would probably have gone mad ages ago if it had not been for my rich imagination. In those times I made images of my wife out of wood and stone, the wife of a husband—also created as a sculpture—who no longer felt any sense of male desire. I could say that the sculptures I made were creatures of romanticism, idealism, and love.

My last works before I divorced from my wife were very popular in the United States. Windy was really surprised. In every letter she asked me why all my sculptures of men were like that. Why they were not complete.

In fact, like many Balinese sculptors, I chose the theme of Lingga and Yoni [the Hindu principle of the male and female energy]. But according to Windy there was a disorder of the soul that radiated from my Lingga. And it was this aberration that made my sculpture sell so well. But even so, Windy kept on asking. I just answered by telling her that I had divorced from my wife and, lo and behold, she replied saying that she had divorced from her husband.

Over time, the business letters gradually transformed into love letters. She said that I should come to the United States for the sake of my career. She would organize an exhibition of statues, paintings, and batik in different cities, in a number of museums. And over there she and I would get married. I replied to her letters full of happiness but with honesty. I told her that I was very much in love with her but that I could not marry her.

Her letter arrived from America, asking me why not. Had my heart already been won over by some Balinese dancer with long dark hair and luscious breasts? In my reply I told her that it had nothing to do with me falling in love with any other woman, whether dancer or goddess, but simply that I could only love my sculpture. Above all else I only felt love for my Windy who, from afar, told me stories constantly and whose breath I felt on my ear at night accompanied by the sound of the waves on Kuta Beach.

Suddenly a letter arrived from her. She would have to accept that my love for her was platonic. That was what she said. Within the next two weeks she would come here. On hearing that, I felt dizzy, as if I had eaten the magic mushrooms that grow out of cow dung on Kuta Beach. But let it be. I did not care if she came or not. Whether we married or not, what did it matter? Whether she was divorced or living as man and wife, whatever. The important thing was that Windy came and saw for herself how things were.

And finally Windy flew from America to Bali. I picked her up at Ngurah Rai airport and took her to my studio, to the place where I lived. That night my nephews and nieces prepared a special meal. After we had eaten with my nephews and nieces, we needed to pour out our hearts to one another, be it in the garden of the house or in one of the bedrooms, for instance mine. But for a sculptor like me who was already married to his sculpture, this was not an easy thing to do. So for a while I felt quite confused and Windy understood. I had to restrain my inner feelings. I felt torn between two courses of action. Should I tell her straight off how I was feeling or hold back? It was a very difficult decision! If I told her right then, a young woman like her would go wandering around this "island of the gods" of ours, end up on Kuta Beach, and find herself a boyfriend before my very eyes. I would get very angry and might even end up killing her. But what then, what would be the point of my life? Even now, what kind of relationship could I have with Windy given that I had just divorced and was now married to my sculpture?

"Windy!" I exclaimed, kissing and hugging her tightly as we sat in the garden in front of my newest piece of sculpture depicting Lingga and Yoni. "We've already made quite a lot of money from my sculpture. I've got a fair bit saved in the bank and you have, too. Wouldn't it be better to just go on a trip around Indonesia? I don't want two lovebirds like us just to be hanging around a place like this. Let's go to Banyuwangi, Surabaya, Malang, Solo, Yogya, Semarang, Cirebon, Bandung, Sukabumi, and Jakarta. I'll take care of all the tickets," I told her.

She seemed to like that idea. "When?"

"Tomorrow. We'll set off tomorrow morning. OK?

"OK," she said kissing me.

That night we talked into the small hours. We talked about art, sculpture, Indonesia and America, about the money to be made selling sculpture, paintings, and batik. But I did not ever tell her my secret, about why the theme of Lingga and Yoni as depicted by me was so distinctive. That night I did not make love to Windy. Windy was really a very special woman to me, a loyal friend apart from our sexual attraction. That made her right for me. I thought that it was only normal for Windy to expect me to follow up on our flirting in the garden surrounded by my pieces of sculpture. But fortunately Windy was a businesswoman, always busy with something. She was an educated woman who didn't really care about what went on in bed, since our kissing session in the garden was enough to satisfy our longing after our long five-year separation.

Even though Windy had fair skin, she still looked very youthful. In my experience, women with fair skin often show their age quickly, especially if they are on their own. But not Windy. She did not paint her lips or her nails, but as soon as I saw her getting off the plane, I noticed that she still had this glow about her. That night, as we sat in the garden, Windy looked even more beautiful.

The light of the moon reflected off her left cheek, and that night she reminded me of a Greek statue.

"If I wasn't so tired, my Windy, I would ask you to model for me tonight. I would ask you to sit nude in my garden and I would make a statue of you out of clay, and a painting. I would demonstrate my artistic genius to you. I believe I am the greatest genius on this earth, because I am inspired by you," I said. Then like a robot, I picked her up and turned her around so that I could look at her from all sides. She laughed happily and, feeling true love, I kissed her, and it was as if all the statues that surrounded us were getting jealous.

"That's enough! We'll make Ketut jealous," I said.

"Who's Ketut?"

"That one!" I pointed at the statue of a Balinese girl. "She was my cook for three months, but then she quit because I refused her advances."

"You're really sick. You're suffering from megalomania. You think that every woman wants you?"

I laughed.

"Did you have a child with her?" asked Windy.

"Balinese women have already learned about family planning from the mobile Government Information Units. They understand how not to get pregnant." I said.

"But you slept with her, right?" said Windy, squeezing my neck and biting my ear. "So you made a statue of your Ketut, did you. Right, tonight, you have to capture this moment forever! That's your punishment for being an unfaithful lover."

"Do you mean it? Aren't you tired?"

"Aren't you tired?"

"No?"

"No!"

"Tonight we'll work all night," said Windy.

That night I asked my assistants to prepare clay. With the moon shining through the coconut trees and sweeping the palms in my garden with its light, before my eyes I truly beheld a Hellenistic beauty.

"When I got off the plane I felt as if my body was being fried by your sun. Only now I feel some relief. Fortunately you made this garden. Did you make this garden especially for your future wife?" asked Windy, already sitting stark naked in the moonlight.

"Yes," I said.

"Who were you thinking about?" she asked. "I bet it was Ketut, wasn't it?"

"No," I replied. "Maybe for Ketut, maybe for Windy, maybe for...Monique," I said enthusiastically.

"Who's she?'

"A girl from Manila," I replied.

"Hm. You've certainly had a lot of women—but very few of them are prepared to become the wife of an artist," said Windy.

"That's right. She got a lot of money selling her body in a Denpasar hotel. Then after she had got her money, she came to me asking me to make a sculpture of her breasts," I said as I turned my focus onto my model, who was enjoying the night air in my garden.

"Did she also know about art?" asked Windy. "I bet she didn't. I don't believe that a prostitute could appreciate art. Women like that are pretty unstable."

"Actually, I believe that women like that plunge themselves into the mystery of life. Unlike us, she is shaken by the mystery, the secrets of this complex life. We artists are aware of this and take up the challenge with our imagination, our intellect, and our intuition. Monique..."

"She's the sort of person who's good at winding someone like you around their little finger," said Windy, in a way that showed that she was feeling jealous.

I quickly washed my hands and dried them on a towel, then approached her as she sat gazing up at the moon. I stroked her hair and kissed her. "You don't need to be jealous, darling. You're the sort of person who has bound me to her for the last five years. In the whole wide world, there's really only you. From a spiritual point of view, I am interested in looking no further, except perhaps from a physical point of view."

"What do you mean?" she asked. "What do you mean by from a physical point of view?"

"I don't mean anything by that. At the end of the day, I believe that in every marriage there is spirituality and physicality, but where in the world do we not find shortcomings and sickness? If the spirit is healthy, the body is sick. If the body is healthy, it's the spirit that's sick. I had that experience in my marriage to my first wife. From a spiritual point of view our relationship was very healthy and very creative, but suddenly physically serious cracks appeared. So finally I chose a marriage of spirituality," I said as I mixed the clay. "Fortunately in the creative process, artists recognize the process of deformation."

"Ngurah, darling," Windy retorted with warmth in her voice.

"What is it, Windy?" I asked with equal warmth.

"I once read all about Luigi Pirandello. He said: 'Art is life's avenger. In artistic creation man becomes God'."

"He becomes a foolish God," I said.

"Why's that?"

"Because he's not able to breathe life into a statue. A human being can only express his ideas through clay. He can halt the transitory nature of life only by making a statue or some other art form. For example, I can only trap your beauty tonight and capture it within my idea of what you are. I reincarnate my idea of you, Windy, through the medium of clay."

"I know, I know, I studied all that stuff at university. Don't go on about it or it starts sounding like a cliché," she said.

I turned on the spotlight which was there precisely for when I worked at night. The effect of the light playing on Windy's body was indeed beautiful, very beautiful! But don't even go there! Don't ever think that faced with the body of a model an artist feels carnal desire. An artist is like a doctor. A doctor looks for illness and gets rid of it, while an artist grasps the impermanence teetering on the edge of the grave, and immortalizes it. I don't believe that an artist feels any great longing for her presence or wants to become God in creating her. I just take the drawing or the map from God so that I can create a bit.

"But maybe it's better like this, Ngurah. Let me remind you of what you asked me five years ago. You asked me to give you a child, right?"

"Yes, I still remember. Back then I was very much in love with you. And I still am."

"Turn off the spotlight for a moment, so that our bodies are lit by the moonlight," said Windy.

"But for now through your body let me give birth to my works of art. Ah! This life is truly absurd. If we get married and have a child, he or she will live for fifty or perhaps seventy years. But if I make a statue of you my work will live on for a thousand years," I said.

I then focused all my creative energy on Windy's body. I mixed the clay and made a nose, eyes, breasts, arms, thighs, cheeks, all out of clay and in accordance with how I saw my model, Windy. I reckon I worked hard that night. Windy just sat still smoking and occasionally drinking coffee. She didn't speak for a long time. The night breeze kept her body cool.

"Windy!" I cried out full of creative passion. "Tonight you are bathed in the light of the moon. Tomorrow you will bathe in the light of the sun on Kuta Beach." Although I spoke these words aloud, I had already become one with the clay.

"Windy! Are you sleepy?" I asked turning off the spotlight. "Why aren't you saying anything?" I noticed that her eyes were still wide open but looking at nothing in particular.

Suddenly Windy said, "Ngurah, it seems as if after being apart for five years, you no longer want to have a child with me. You've changed. I'm afraid that someone fundamentally different is beside me."

"You don't need to be afraid," I said. "My heart is totally yours."

"Ah! That's what men everywhere say. They say that it's women who are the crafty ones. The craftiness of women is just how they fill the lives of men, but the craftiness of men is in the way in which they take a woman to the heavens, raise her hopes like kites in the sky and then let go of the string. Millions of women on this earth end up becoming prostitutes all because of the craftiness of men. You just want to make a statue out of me, while five years ago you wanted me to become your wife," she said, then stood up, wrapped her batik cloth around her body, and strode off towards the sitting room (she is actually quite tall) where she collapsed onto the sofa. She was crying.

I felt dazed. I paced around the sitting room, not knowing what I should say. Ah! Stop being so stupid and open up your heart to her, I thought. So I sat down. I pushed my bottom into her back and began to caress her reddish brown hair. "It's better that I'm straight with you." I said.

"I already understand. Ketut is the only one your heart cares about."

I just kept sitting and caressing her hair. We did not speak for a long time, as I was waiting for her to calm down a bit. Then when the time was right, I started speaking very softly and as carefully as possible. "Windy, would we marry in accordance with Indonesian law?" I asked.

She did not reply. I am a person who likes to use techniques designed to attract attention when I start talking to them. I was not sure what this would achieve, but ultimately I hoped that there would be a dialogue and that we would come to understand each other.

Windy still did not speak for a while, but then she turned round and put her hand on my thigh. "I really love you, Ngurah. In my previous marriage I kept mentioning Bali and the name Ngurah, so much so that my former husband got jealous and asked for a divorce."

Such words made me feel confused. "OK," I said. "Tonight I must thank you. I would ask you just to listen to me with your full attention, and please don't get too emotional. I was born in a village called Pelaga, in the interior of Bali, far away from a lifestyle where sex had been commercialized. For us, sex was something sacred. So sacred that there was the culture of Lingga and Yoni. No doubt you have heard of phallic culture, right? But since I was a small boy until now I have taken no notice of this. I was never circumcised, and because I rarely washed my body, I got cancer. In Bali there have been several cases of carcinomas of the penis, including me. Because of that, a special doctor amputated my penis and I am now among the people who no longer have this organ. My body is like a statue whose form has been changed. My body has been deformed in a strange way, darling. I'm sure I'm right in thinking that you cannot take a man as your husband who has become like a statue?" I told Windy with a heavy heart. My voice was hoarse, and full of emotion. "Now sometimes I go with the mobile Family Planning Units to help them in their campaign to encourage people not to have too many children. Alongside the Family Planning campaign I give out information to men and boys about the importance of being clean, so that they don't end up with a carcinoma of the penis!"

Windy got up suddenly from the sofa and hugged me. I thought she saw the hopelessness of the situation and wanted to strangle me, but then I heard her say: "I don't need that. I need you."

The Absent-minded Lawyer

The airport taxi dropped Dewi, together with her husband and two small children, at their grandfather's house. The two of them sat down and she announced: "We've come to look for work here, Grandfather. In the outlying provinces it's very difficult for law graduates like us to get a job."

Grandfather was alarmed. "But it's a long way to fly to look for work. So, you two are law graduates, are you. But whose going to look after your land?"

"Oh, Grandfather. Because of the long dry season all the fields are dry. Fortunately we still have Palmyra, cabbage palms and coconut trees so we can use the sap. Every day we make sugar, drink the sap and liquid sugar and make vinegar *lawar* [mixed vegetables] out of papaya leaves, moringa, and seaweed, and mix it with fish, shellfish, and octopus which we get at low tide when they get caught in the stone bunds made by our great-grandfather. We're satisfied, we don't feel like we're in a time of famine because there is always something to eat, but the children are always crying and asking for rice and bread. I fool the children by splitting open the coconuts which have already sprouted. Inside them there's stuff which is a bit like bread," Dewi explained.

"Oh my, by the grace of God, the universities spawn thousands of law graduates every year but they are like chicks cheeping with hunger because there's no work," grumbled Grandfather. "It looks like the only ones who have any use for lawyers are the corrupt.

Hah, if there were no corrupt people, the lawyers of this country would be finished," complained Grandfather. Then he laughed out loud.

"But in the outlying provinces there are not many corrupt people, Grandfather. If there were, there would be lots of work for us defending them," said Dewi, also laughing.

"Oh, there are plenty of corrupt people in this city, my granddaughter," said Grandfather.

"If that's the case, do you think your granddaughter can find work defending the corrupt, Grandfather?" asked Dewi.

"Don't defend the corrupt, wipe them out with high fees!" said Grandfather as he struggled to remember something. "Oh, I have just remembered. Back then my older sister, your great-aunt, as a young woman would go shopping in the market every day. There at the market was a child of about seven, sleeping on the floor of the market because he had missed his boat and could not get home. The child was begging. Your great-aunt took him home, bathed him, gave him new clothes and some good food, then sent him to school. From elementary school through senior high school. Then he went off and eventually graduated as a lawyer. Later he became a judge. But then he stopped doing this when a businessman paid him a bribe, and with that money he was able to buy a piece of land for planting pineapples. On this land he built a factory to can pineapples for both export and domestic consumption. But the factory burned down and there were problems with the land so he went bankrupt. Then he opened a law firm. His business is thriving because corruption is on the up. If you'd like to work in a law firm, I'm sure this adopted grandson of ours would take you on."

"We'd love to. When our great-aunt went blind, we didn't know that she had an adopted son who had become a success. Now Great Aunt is ninety. She's blind but her body is still strong. She eats normally, but all she remembers is life in her home village. Every day she rambles on about what it was like growing up in the village. But inevitably Great Aunt's body is deteriorating. She can no longer control her bowel movements so she has become incontinent. She shits herself every morning. And boy, there's piles of it. She eats a lot of meat, as she still has all her teeth. But it means we have to take Great Aunt to the toilet to wash her," Dewi reported.

"Oh, God. Living a long time complicates life for the grandchildren," said Grandfather.

"There are too many unemployed law graduates in the town where we were born. If it's too difficult to become a lawyer, they just become security guards; the main thing is there's a salary coming in every month. But the fact is there are plenty of corrupt people in the capital city who need lawyers to defend them, while in the outlying provinces there really is very little corruption, but there are plenty of law graduates and lawyers. So we took the decision to move. Because we need to help our mother, as we're not able to afford to employ a maid yet to help her look after our great-aunt," said Dewi.

So not long afterwards Grandfather took Dewi and her husband to the law office of their great-aunt's adopted son.

Lawyer Lell Hanack looked pleased to see them. Hearing them talk about their great-aunt's condition, he was shocked. "If I had known that Great Aunt was still alive at the age of ninety and was blind, I would have put her in an old people's home. As I was so busy with my work, I had forgotten to ask after her. In fact I'm getting more and more forgetful. There are just so many corrupt people and so much work defending them that I don't get enough sleep, and my brain is going to seed."

Dewi and her husband were taken on by this firm. Besides working as lawyers, Dewi's husband became Lell's personal driver and Dewi was taken on as his secretary. They were very happy, as there were lots of corrupt people seeking their services. The corruption industry provided them with employment night and day.

Suddenly there arose a case of slander against Lell Hanack, saying that he had a false law degree. Someone came forward who had known Lell when he was at university. He claimed that he had only taken the last semester of the course in the law faculty. In fact faculties that needed funds had offered those who could pay the money the chance to just study for one semester and then graduate as a lawyer under false pretenses.

But the story of how Lell Hanack managed to get one over on the capital city was very interesting. When he finished school, he bragged that he would be able to get to the capital without any money. And he achieved this by boarding a vessel transporting cattle and their fodder while they were loading up, and hiding in the piles of grass. All he had with him was a sharp knife. Because he was a stowaway he did not get any food, so every night he would creep out of the piles of grass, cut off the ear of one of the cows and eat it raw.

Once he got off the ship, he did his best to hold his own in the big city by learning to sleep on his feet but to never stand still. And as he slept on his feet, he mumbled prayers to ward off thieves and other evils that might befall him. Then he got a job as a watchman that paid him a decent salary.

The funny thing was, besides becoming adept at sleeping on his feet while mumbling prayers, he also learned how to behave like a transvestite and got himself work in a beauty salon for several months. He learned about this work from a satirical poster on the university campus which said: *Want to get a job with a good salary? Practice wiggling your hips and waving your arms. Once you can do a good imitation of a transvestite, just apply to our salon. You're sure of being accepted.* But after working there for a while he started fearing permanent damage to his anus and getting AIDS, so he went back to being a real man who slept on his feet while mumbling prayers. With that work, he really did complete law school. So he was a genuine law graduate, not someone who had graduated in just one semester.

Perhaps it was because he had so much work but he really did not get enough sleep. He started to get sick, although he still appeared to be healthy. Maybe his brain got weak from having to defend so many corrupt people to the point that he became very absent-minded. It was only after struggling for a long time for something that he had forgotten that he would remember it again.

One day Dewi got the surprise of her life when Lell Hanack walked into her office wearing only his underpants. He asked her, "Dewi, where have you put my trousers?"

Naturally Dewi did not know what to say. Because she did not answer him straight away, Lell Hanack got annoyed. "You want to become a pretty woman who can make millions of rupiah from corrupt people, so you hide my trousers, is that it?"

Suddenly an employee came in carrying his trousers. "Here, Boss, you left these in the bathroom."

"Oh, sorry, I forgot."

That was the first example of her boss's forgetfulness that Dewi experienced.

One day, Herman, Dewi's husband, was taking his boss home from the courthouse. They got stuck in a traffic jam.

"Ah, when is this country going to be rid of these traffic jams?" grumbled the boss.

"The government needs to introduce a new transmigration program, and give money to engineers and farmers to encourage the maximum number of people to move to and develop the areas where there's empty land," said Herman. "The solution is to empty Jakarta so that there are only one million people left. Arrange for nine million to transmigrate. That's the solution. Indonesia is huge.

And so is its ocean. So Bajo people who love the forest live on the sea."

"That's up to the minister of transmigration! Just focus on finding us a way out of this traffic jam," said the lawyer.

"The most important thing is to be patient. The roads these days are packed with vehicles. The big city teaches us to be packed with patience," said Herman.

"For anyone who is not a driver, it's clear that we need make a U-turn. For a driver to make a U-turn, that's fine. For a lawyer to make a U-turn, that's immoral. But if a driver makes a U-turn he's honest. So if we get stuck in a traffic jam like this, turn round and go back," said Lell Hanack. "Come on! Just do a U-turn so that we can get out of this traffic jam," ordered the lawyer.

"But how can we, sir? There's no sign that says we can make a U-turn," replied Herman.

"Huh! This country is finished because you can't make a U-turn!" complained the lawyer.

Herman just kept looking in front of him without saying anything, searching for a sign that indicated that they could do a U-turn. The lawyer opened the car door and walked off in the opposite direction. Herman was alarmed to see his boss leaping from the top of one car to the next. Drivers blew their horns. When Herman got home he found to his surprise that Lell Hanack had got back before him.

As Dewi and Herman's financial position started to improve, their relationship began to become strained, because a friend had said that Herman and his boss were often seen at the sauna bath. Herman denied this, saying that he always waited for his boss in the car.

One day Herman was sitting quietly in the office in front of his wife's desk when Lell Hanack came in. With an absent-minded look on his face, he rudely pointed his finger at Herman and shouted: "What's this person doing sitting here? This is not your office, this is a lawyer's office. Please leave, I am not taking on any new staff. Out!"

Dewi and Herman were shocked, although they realized that Lell Hanack was becoming more and more absent-minded as time went on, starting from the time that he forgot that he had left his trousers in the bathroom, and the time when he wanted Herman to do a U-turn, got out of their vehicle, and began jumping like Spiderman from car to car.

Several months later, having eaten a lot of jackfruit and bread for lunch, he went to the toilet to have a shit. Sitting on the toilet he had a terrible struggle because the feces were too hard to come out. He sat there straining to move his bowels for hours but the feces just would not come out. Finally all strength left him, he breathed his last, and died on the toilet.

When I Became a Papuan

The white boat was carrying a hundred political prisoners along the river to the headwaters, some sixty kilometers from the estuary. Because the river was deep and the current was not too strong, the journey did not take long. Amongst the hundred of us, I was the most daring. I was the one who dared to jump from the boat in the dark night. I swam underwater for a while, and as I did so I heard repeated shots, but luckily none of the bullets hit me. When I eventually came to the surface, gasping for air, I saw that the boat was already far away. The shooting had stopped. Maybe the shooters had consigned me to the crocodiles of which there were many in the rivers of Papua, or maybe they thought I had been strangled by one of those large snakes, as big as those in the rivers in Brazil.

Half alive and half dead in that river, I swam to the river bank and looked for a fallen tree trunk or a branch that I could sleep on. I climbed a large tree by holding onto its aerial roots and crawled to a tree trunk that was growing horizontally. As the tree trunk was quite big, I was able to stretch out my body, and soon I was fast asleep in the Papuan jungle. When I woke up the next morning, I saw that I had what looked like black stockings on my feet, but in fact all I had on was a pair of shorts. Then I realized that they were not stockings at all but swarms of black mosquitoes. Probably anybody else would have felt itchy, but because when I was small I lived in the fields in the middle of a forest, I was used to the itching and the discomfort of mosquito bites. Even though my skin felt itchy, I just put up with it until the sun gradually began to rise in the east and rays of sunlight penetrated the thick foliage of the trees. My body felt better and better as it lapped up the sunlight. The calling of the birds of paradise and the sound of the monkeys were bidding me a warm welcome. Then they invited me to have breakfast. I climbed up to a higher branch where the monkeys were having their breakfast and they let me pick some of the fresh fruit that they were eating. I was soon full. Then I sought out some hot sunlight to warm my body and dry out my clothes.

Once my clothes were dry, I began to think about how I was going to find my lunch so that I did not starve and I could stay healthy. I saw a lot of turtledoves flying among the birds of paradise, so I searched for rocks to throw at these birds. Ever since I was small I had practiced throwing stones. And even as a grown man I still ate bird meat every day. I picked up ten stones and killed ten turtledoves—but the problem then was how to cook them. But I was clever enough to find a way since as a boy I was used to making fires, as I used to work as a shepherd and I was used to making my own fire from the twigs and dry wood that I found on dead tree trunks. So with the twigs of dry wood I found, I made a small campfire in the middle of the forest and roasted the turtledoves right there. I filled my stomach with all ten of them. Then I walked a long way from my campfire when suddenly I saw several clumps of banana trees which had quite a lot of fruit on them. I climbed up one of them and picked the ripe fruit and I roasted the half-ripe ones. Meanwhile I killed several more birds to eat with the bananas.

After all that food I felt really full and began to get sleepy, so I slept on an upper branch of a horizontal tree. When I woke up, I was thirsty; but I was worried about drinking the river water as it was not very clear. I walked on a bit and suddenly saw amidst the other trees a few coconut palms. Oh Papua! My heart cried out. Why hadn't I been born here, why had I been born far away from here on an island where only savannah grass grew and people labored hard to cultivate bananas and coconut palms. Here in Papua, coconut palms, bananas, and other fruit just grew naturally. It crossed my mind that God loved the people of Papua more than other Indonesians. After assuaging my thirst, I continued my journey along the river, and suddenly I saw some stones that were sharp and flat and others that were pointed. I quickly picked up a sharp one to make an axe, then I found a clump of bamboo and busied myself making a bow and arrow, so that I could live from shooting animals like wild boar and was also able to defend myself. Then I created a snare from string made from tree bark.

It was already nearly nightfall, so after my dinner of turtledove, banana, and coconut water, I jumped up again into my tree and slept up there until morning with my axe and my bow and arrow beside me. When I woke up in the morning I saw a medium-sized wild pig suspended in my trap and squealing loudly. Maybe this had been going on all night, but because I was so tired and had slept so soundly, I had only just seen my success. I promised myself that I would never again sleep so soundly that I was not aware of the sounds of the forest all around me.

I immediately began to cut up the wild pig up with my axe and the other knife-like stones and roasted it. After it was cooked, I tied it up with string so that it could not be carried off by a monkey or any other creature. Then I looked for leaves that had a salty or sour taste to give flavor to my food. By chance there were lots of chillis on scrubby bushes under the trees; the seeds had come from bird droppings. Walking on another few hundred meters, I suddenly came upon breadfruit and durian trees laden with fruit. I cheered with joy. "I've found bread in the trees and as chance would have it there's butter too hanging from my tree. Thank you,

God, thank you." I got on my knees and prayed. All at once a bird perched on my head, singing melodiously, and I had the feeling that it was conveying the spirit of abundant love from our Lord. I immediately picked several breadfruit and durian and carried them to my campfire. I roasted the breadfruit and ate this bread with butter made from wild boar fat. Oh Papua, you're providing such luxuries as were sought out by the King of England when he sent an expedition to the Pacific Islands in search of breadfruit so that the English would not have to tire themselves out ploughing fields of wheat.

As I was having my meal, suddenly I found myself surrounded by a group of Papuans shouting and pointing their spears and bows and arrows at me. The shouting ceased when a voice told them to stop. It seemed like that voice belonged to the chief of the tribe. He approached me and asked in Indonesian, "Where are you from, brother?"

"I escaped from the white boat, I'm a political prisoner. I got caught for fighting for independence. I jumped into the river in the middle of the night. It was the colonial government who arrested me."

"To hell with the government! We are free men who do not want to be bothered by these colonizers. We are the legal owners of the land of Papua. If you're a good man, we will adopt you as one of our own. How about it?"

I sprang down to kiss his feet. "Thank you, thank you, Chief of the Tribe." Then he pulled me up and kissed me. Although he smelled different to me, I was still pleased to take in his scent.

That day we had a party. They brought sago and cassava and a big pig, and then we made a *batu bakar* [burning stone] ceremony. Afterwards they took me with them to their village, to a house which sat on thirty-meter-high stilts. I was told to take a rest and they left me there.

I slept very soundly. When I woke up my body felt refreshed—but I was astonished at what I saw before me. By the hearth a young girl was breastfeeding her darling, a piglet. She smiled at me and I was forced to smile back. Then a small child who was still of breastfeeding age, who had been fast asleep beside her, woke up and began crying. She put down the piglet, and picked up the child and put her on her breast to feed. As she was breastfeeding the child, suddenly it began to rain and a dog in the space underneath the house started to bark. She got up nimbly and brought me the baby and I held her, rocking her in my arms. The baby seemed happy. The young woman skillfully climbed down the ladder, which wasn't really a ladder but more a trunk of wood as big as a human thigh, with notches cut into it for rungs. She went down the thirty meters and came up again carrying her beloved dog. But I was taken aback as she didn't just climb up again with a dog but also with an adult pig which she had put in a net hanging from her head. The pig was snoring gently as it lay against the woman's back.

I took a deep breath. Entering such a different world filled me with amazement. Just imagine living in a house thirty meters off the ground with three human beings and three animals. In this raised house, people eat and then piss and shit through gaps in the planks. The same goes for the animals. The Papuan people are not azoic creatures, they are not a society without animals. People without animals are city creatures, who spend their time encased between walls so they lose their sense of being animals themselves. If you think about it, this animal quality is actually closely related to our humanity, and so the city people who live in stone boxes high up in the sky can easily maltreat their maids, especially those from Indonesia, and you often hear stories of maids committing suicide by throwing themselves out of the boxes situated hundreds of meters up in the air. In this Papuan forest, the Papuan people love the forest, and the people and the animals all make a living together from the forest.

So I felt calmer when I thought like this. I was sure that because the Papuans were kind to animals, they would be kind to other human beings like them, even if that human being was a foreigner like me.

"Can you speak Indonesian?" I asked.

"I can speak the Papuan dialect of Malay," she answered.

My heart rejoiced. All around the country, people say, there is Ambon Malay, Manado Malay, Malaysian Malay and so on. I'm thankful that everyone can still communicate with each other well. As we chatted, the woman told me that her husband had died. I was shocked when she showed me her hand and I saw her fingers. "Our tradition dictates that if someone in the family dies we have to cut off one of our fingers and bury it with the deceased."

I did not say anything. I felt alarmed. Of course she would have cried, both because she was in pain and because she was sad. But she got on with cooking and seeing to all my needs. After she became my wife, she took a kind of gourd and made it into a *koteka* [penis gourd]. Once it was dry I wore it. The only problem was that my skin was pale like the *lansium* fruit. It would have been much better if my skin had been black!

For that to happen, I needed to labor under the hot sun. Fortunately in our thirty-meter-high house I found an axe and a machete. Every day I busied myself making a long slender dugout from the trunk of a tall tree that I had felled beside the fields. As time went on my skin got darker and darker. That just left my hair. My hair needed to be curly, but that was easy to achieve: my wife and I used the ammonia from our urine, so my hair went frizzy. I looked at my face and my body and my hair in a mirror which I had bought from an old woman in exchange for five pigs. When I saw how much I looked like a real Papuan, I started to have the ambition to become the head of the tribe. Or even better to become the king of the Papuan jungle. My wife agreed with me. She took the tusk of a wild boar and stuck it through my nose. Strings of gleaming boar's teeth were hung from my ears.

After a year, my wife told me that she was expecting our first child. I was very happy. I was sure my child would be very healthy, as every day I saw that my wife's breasts were getting bigger and bigger, hanging down over her pregnant belly like two long black papaya fruit. Once my dugout was ready, my wife and I would both row it on the river. Because there was no salt, we paddled to the estuary, to the beach on the open sea. There we collected water in bowls made of a type of gourd, and when the water evaporated we had salt. We took that salt back to use ourselves and to exchange for chicken or piglets.

My wife and I worked hard every day in the heat of the sun to clear the fields for cultivation. We cut down the grass and the trees and burned it all, leaving our field clean and ready for planting. Papuan soil is very fertile so it doesn't have to be hoed like in Java or other islands. We planted our land with corn, gourd, chilli, cassava, and sweet potato. Soon we were living off the vegetables that we had planted. From our thirty-meter-high house we watched over our fertile land. One thing that amazed me, though, was the rain and the strong wind with lightening and the sound of thunder claps all around us, our house swaying in the strong wind. My eyes would open wide with fear and my body would shrink at the sound of lightening splitting the earth. Luckily near our house there were a few large trees which were more than fifty meters high, and the lightening used to like to strike these trees. One week later one of those trees had withered and died.

The rain storms and lightening disappeared, and some three or four months later the corn and other vegetables were growing in abundance. My wife and I harvested them and took them to the market in a well-known place called Tapol Village, meaning the village of political prisoners. It was lucky that there was a village like this in the middle of the jungle, with a market, military and police barracks, plus office workers, shops, and a hospital.

Because I had already metamorphosed into a real Papuan man, the security forces did not recognize me as the political prisoner who had plunged into that dangerous river. I was believed to be the chief of the tribe because of the way my face was decorated and the long tusk in my nose.

When we had finished selling our produce, my wife and I paddled our dugout back to our house in the sky. Once the harvest was finished, there was a big burning stone party with all our neighbors from the surrounding fields who also lived in houses on stilts thirty meters high.

One day, when her pregnancy was already at an advanced stage and she was about to give birth, my wife suddenly went down the ladder. I watched from above, asking myself where my beloved wife was going. Then she wrapped her arms around one of the poles. At the foot of the pole there was dried straw. Then she stopped hugging the pole and pushed it so hard that the house moved as if it was being blown by the wind. Oh God, I watched as my child slipped out of her and dropped onto the fresh straw below. Then I heard the sound of a baby crying. Like Tarzan I jumped up and slid down the ladder which was really only one tree trunk to pick up my newborn baby. The amazing thing was that my wife was behaving as if nothing had happened. She asked me to go and get the basket which we had already prepared, put the baby in it, and took it upstairs.

I immediately heated up a sharp knife, waited until it had cooled down, then cut the umbilical cord. Extraordinary! My wife did not need a doctor, a midwife, or even any medicine. As it happened, our fields were full of nutritious foods so my wife's breast milk was sufficient, even too much for the baby, so she also shared it with a piglet. I immediately told our neighbors the news and they shared in our happiness. Then I held a burning stone party, and we celebrated by killing two pigs to eat and with dancing around the bonfire.

A few years on I realize I am living in the Stone Age; but, although that is the case, I always have enough to eat. I am not some unemployed person like so many in the modern world. In this Papuan jungle, people can eat their fill every day. There is no famine, no one will be a poor person without enough to eat or a vagrant with no home who has to live under a bridge in one of the big cities. Here I am self-sufficient; my life depends unconditionally on the land and the forest. Satan, known as money, cannot tempt me here. I seek money as I please, paddling our boat to the market as if we were going on a picnic. If we don't sell our produce, I take it home and give it to the pigs. The pigs are my bank where I have my savings.

What I fear is getting ill—but because we eat so nutritiously I hope that I will stay healthy, unlike some people in the village in times gone by who suffered from elephantiasis. But supposing I did get that, I am sure that it would have been caused by Mother Papua who did not want me to leave. And supposing I ever was afflicted by elephantiasis, then I would thank Mother Papua for not wanting me to leave this prosperous Papuan jungle!

Once our child started to walk and could climb up and down alone, my wife and I were very happy. We were always laughing at how lively and cute our child was. He was like a little monkey, although his skin color was like mine, with a light golden tinge. His hair was curly. My wife just laughed and laughed... laughing to herself, although there was nothing funny about our child. I joined in with the laughter every day, even though this world and this jungle did not really have much in it to laugh about.

It felt as if we were afflicted with a laughing sickness. We never stopped laughing, even if there was nothing funny to laugh at. We laughed as we loaded our produce into the dugout, we laughed as we paddled our boat as far as the market in the village of political prisoners. We laughed not because we made a big profit on our produce, we just laughed because we laughed. We didn't ask ourselves why we were laughing all day except for when we were tired and sleepy so our laugh went to sleep with us. When we woke up in the morning we laughed some more. Then we were tired and went to sleep, and when we woke up once again we laughed some more....

There was a member of the hospital staff who saw our behavior and took us to the hospital. We laughed all the way there. On meeting the doctor we just kept laughing. And I was shocked to bits when the doctor said, "It's probably because you eat a lot of pork at the burning stone parties. The meat is not cooked through, so the tapeworms are still alive. Then the tapeworms enter the bloodstream, crawl into the brain, and damage the nerve that controls laughter in the brain. The worms live there and if those worms laugh, then you will laugh too."

I said to myself, "Better to be afflicted by elephantiasis than to be colonized by tapeworms!" My wife, our two children, and I were all admitted into hospital as in-patients. Because I was not in the sun for a long time, my skin turned pale and my hair went straight again. I was recognized and arrested straight away as a political prisoner. Living in the prison in Tapol Village is not at all the same thing as living in a house high up in the sky. It is more organized, but not life as an independent, free human being. It is after all called Tapol, for political prisoners.

Sesandu

My name is Immanuel, but ever since I was a little boy, people have called me Nuel. I was the fruit of the womb of a woman called Rose from Rote, a small island in the very south of our republic. My mother married a second-hand clothes peddler from South Sulawesi. When I was only three years old, my father was swallowed up by the sea in the Pukuafu Straits between Timor and Rote. I can recall things clearly only from the age of about five or six. I remembered how my mother would take me from village to village on foot, selling second-hand clothes. If there was no money, she bartered second-hand clothes for rice, corn, and sugar. As we travelled around, if my mother had managed to get sugar she gave me some; if I was thirsty she gave me the sap of the Palmyra palm and I drank my fill. What I loved eating most were *kue cucur*, fried cakes made of rice flour and sugar. I got to eat those when my mother managed to sell some second-hand clothes. But the really healthy food was corn mixed with sugar and mung beans dry-fried without oil. Mother and I often got tired walking from village to village, and when we couldn't go any further we just lay down and slept on the grass at the side of the road, oblivious to the hot sun burning our skin.

Another happy memory was when I was first taken to school. I was overjoyed. I faintly remember my mother saying, "May my son be famous one day…"

But when I was in my fourth year of school, my mother died of lung cancer. I think what caused my mother's death was her habit of chewing betelnut and her mouth would be full of tobacco hanging from her lips.

After that my uncle came from Kupang to collect me, as our relatives from Rote had moved to the island of Timor to cultivate the land in the interior, where for centuries the people of Rote had had a number of settlements. My mother had two siblings. Her older sister lived in Bali and the eldest, a brother, in Kupang. Her brother had two hectares of land and on it there were many Palmyra palms growing. To begin with my uncle lived by tapping the palm trees, boiling the sap until it became sugar, and then selling it at the market in Kupang. But then all at once, as he observed the palm leaves swaying and singing in the dry season wind, he came upon the idea of making *sesandu*. The Javanese call this stringed musical instrument "*sesando*" with an "o" but the people of Rote call it "sesandu," and it is even spelled like that in books written in English about Rote.

My uncle's name was Eduard but everyone called him Edu. Uncle Edu was a very talented musician. He played the sesandu at parties, and if there were no parties he just played on his own for hours and hours. But after he became a craftsman who made sesandu, he would be busy for hours and hours, indeed days and days, making these musical instruments. There was a gong sesandu which had only nine strings, and there was also a viola sesandu which had several octaves so that one could even play Mozart on it.

I became his assistant. I climbed up the palms and cut the leaves, I sawed up the wood and bamboo, I delivered the sesandu that people ordered, and I became his favorite nephew. My uncle put me through school until my fifth year, but because I was more interested in becoming a sesandu-maker, I often played truant and eventually dropped out of school. I transferred from a formal school to an informal one, the sesandu school. In the end I became both a sesandu-player and a sesandu-maker. From when I was quite small I was able to make quite a lot of money. Besides what I earned making sesandu, I had a contract to play at a star-rated hotel in Kupang, so I did not have to struggle like friends my age who always had empty pockets.

But that sense of pride in being someone who could make his own living gradually disappeared. When I was about fifteen years old, I saw all my friends going to school and felt embarrassed, as I had stopped studying at primary school level. Besides, on a number of occasions when I finished my sesandu sessions, people would ask me where I went to school. I would frequently lie and say I was studying at university. They would often then ask what I was studying and I would say: music.

Then my mother's older sister arrived unexpectedly from Bali. When she discovered that I had dropped out of school at primary level, she grumbled. She complained to my uncle and his wife, asking them why they had neglected my formal education, when there were schools everywhere.

Then my aunt said, "You just come to Bali with me. You can live in Denpasar and work in my hotel. Every evening you can play the sesandu in the restaurant and earn a salary. But during the day you must go back to school, OK? You start by doing your primary school exam, then proceed to junior high school and continue your education until you graduate from college."

No kidding, I was a happy boy.

"Listen to me, in the old days there were not as many schools as now, so your mother and I and even your uncle could not get much of an education. But now, there are schools everywhere. You only need to walk a few paces and there's a school right in front of you," said my mother's older sister.

So when she had had enough of holidaying in Rote, she returned to Kupang, and the two of us took a plane to Bali, carrying a couple of sesandu and some other ethnic Rote instruments like the gong and the drum and a few other musical instruments. Also a few bags of smoked dried buffalo meat, which is called *daging se'i*. And we did not forget to take tamarind with us, or *tambring Timor* as we call it, which grows wild on the savannah.

In Denpasar I was astonished to see how developed my mother's sister's business was. My mother's older sister, my aunt, my own auntie! Now she owned a big building, a garment factory with a hundred people sewing there. The profit made from this garment factory had been used to buy a hotel with a swimming pool and a restaurant. In the restaurant there was an area for music and dancing. Extraordinary. Before I started playing music, I was told to get my driving license, for although she already had her own driver, she wanted me to be able to drive the car around to run different errands and even to drive myself to and from school.

Her business had started at about the time when my father died. While my mother was travelling around from village to village with her second-hand clothes, my aunt started with one needle. Rather than traipsing around all over the place, she would just sit in one place, embroidering pillow cases. To start with it was just two pillow cases, and a lady neighbor bought them both. This lady showed them to a Dutch tourist and the tourist was so interested that he ordered a few. There followed orders for ten, then twenty, then a hundred, then two hundred, then a thousand. So my aunt ordered sewing machines, enough for a garment factory and a boutique. She started out small and gradually got bigger and bigger. She was very proud of her business. "I dropped out of school in the first year of elementary school, but, see, starting from just one needle, I now own a factory and a hotel."

I reflected that it was a bit like that for my uncle. He started out with a machete and a knife, a small saw, and a small drill. He had gone from having just a few simple tools to owning a workshop making sesandu. Nearly all the family members from both my father's and mother's side had moved away from the island. That had been happening gradually when something terrible happened to our family. One of my grandfather's nephews embarrassed the whole family by doing something which was certainly not in line with our customs.

It's a sad story. When my father's cousin proposed to a girl from Rote, the girl's parents asked for a dowry that was truly excessive: forty buffalos, forty cows, forty horses, forty grams of gold chains, and forty million rupiah in cash! My father's cousin's family asked if they could pay the dowry in instalments over forty years, as was customary in Rote, but the girl's family refused. It had to be paid up front. It was impossible for them to do this, as the boy's family owned only ten *mamar* (plots of land with coconut palms) and some rice fields and nowhere near the number of buffalos, cows, and horses that they were asking for. So his proposal was rejected. Who would have suspected: one night my father's cousin took a machete and killed forty of the girl's family members, including his own fiancée. There was a huge uproar. Rote Island became known as "the island of murderers." It was very shameful.

So to avoid the vengeance that would follow such an incident, my relatives moved to Timor. As it happened, on Timor there was lots of unoccupied land. The people native to Timor preferred living on the high ground, on the slopes or on the top of the hills, where there was a strong wind to keep away the mosquitos. The people of Rote could not live far from a river or a spring. As long as they had water, they would have wealth in abundance. They made rice fields, and planted hardy trees like coconut, jackfruit, breadfruit, areca nut, and such like. Such a garden area was known as a *mamar*. So a *mamar* became an ecological garden. One often heard a dowry referred to as a *belis* or a *mamar*. One or two *mamar* were enough to "exchange" for a girl's hand in marriage. My family moved to Timor and became rich and prosperous, as they owned *mamar* and rice fields and reared horses, cattle, goats, sheep, and pigs. And lots of chickens. But some of those who moved from Rote to Timor were not of good character and behaved dishonestly. Cows, buffalos, and horses belonging to the people of Timor, which roamed free in the fields and always went down to the water to drink, were surreptitiously branded with the letter R burnt onto their backsides, which could never be removed. That meant that they became the property of the people from Rote. Fortunately I was not living in that village, although I had been asked to become a herdsman with them.

My dear aunt was also invited to stay in that village on the plains with the other people from Rote, but soon a soldier from Bali asked for her hand in marriage. I am grateful to my aunt's husband, for although his wife had dropped out of school in the first year of elementary school, he assiduously taught her arithmetic, and I was amazed to see how well she could add up, subtract, divide and so forth. My aunt was very talented at mathematics. Her mind was like a computer. That was what made her such a successful businesswoman.

Although she only completed the first year of formal schooling, when her employees married they would say that they had graduated from a tourism academy. And why was that? The girls who worked with her would become skillful and industrious housewives. My aunt told us about when she was an adolescent. One Dutch controller (now known as regent/*bupati*) gathered together a group of young adolescent girls. They were taught to sew, embroider, wash clothes, bleach white clothes by washing them in soap and then laying them out on the grass, iron, and fold up the clothes and arrange them in the cupboard. They were taught the art of managing the kitchen. The kitchen had to be spotless. The plates and bowls had to be washed and dried up and placed neatly on the shelves. The pantry had to be clean and free of flies and termites, the kitchen walls needed to be kept white, the table needed to be scrubbed with soap and water. Everything about the way in which they arranged the table, the plates, the cutlery, and the napkins had to be clean and tidy. Drinking water had to be boiled; vegetables, fish, and meat had to be fresh and washed. And of course the floor had to be mopped and the mattresses had to be aired once a week, and when they ate they should not clatter the dishes or leave any rice on their plates, and so it went on. In short, all households should be organized like a star-rated hotel.

In the end all these young girls received marriage proposals from teachers, office workers, policemen, soldiers, and businessmen. These were the young girls who had received their education from the wife of the controller. And among them was my aunt. Although she dropped out of school in the first year of elementary school, her knowledge of how to run a household was equivalent to that obtained at a finishing school. It may not have been a formal education, but it was an informal education, like an apprenticeship.

Seeing how some Papuans were still wearing penis gourds (*koteka*) and living in the forest, my aunt flew there and brought back ten children to undertake an apprenticeship in her business. She taught them how to wash three times a day with soap, how to dress properly, how to eat at table with proper table manners, and such things. Because there is such a lot of wood in Papua, my aunt set up a workshop and they learned how to make modern houses (*honai* in Papuan) which were clean and healthy. She suggested that later they could build their own houses on land below a spring so that they could have running water in their houses; they were taught to construct a clean bathroom with a clean toilet that could be flushed, and many more such things. They were taught to make a waterwheel which turned a dynamo and a windmill to pump out water from the well or the river. In short, my aunt taught them to become village leaders who could become regents and or occupy other posts in the village government structure if they wanted to.

My aunt always took a deep breath when she said that if every regent/*bupati* had a wife who did what the wife of this controller had done, it would not have taken the Papuans a century to get educated like the people of developed nations. But that was my aunt, a village woman who started her business with one needle and a circle of embroidery. My aunt, who dropped out of formal schooling in the first year but took up every opportunity of non-formal education to the extent that now she had her own garment factory and hotel.

Every evening I played the sesandu in her restaurant. Then I was allowed to sleep until ten o'clock in the morning. I woke up refreshed, took a bath, and then helped with some light chores, then had lunch and got ready for school. First I passed the primary school exam so I could go on to junior high school. Then I studied for three years to get my junior high school certificate, and then after another three years, I finished senior high school. My aunt proposed that I study music at university.

To cut a long story short, I graduated in musicology. I still went on playing the sesandu at my aunt's hotel as usual. I played and sang. Out of the blue, an American female journalist asked to interview me. Oh, I was so happy. I willingly answered all her questions. Then not long afterwards, the journalist brought me a copy of that famous newspaper, *The New York Times*. There on the page was my face, there was my beloved sesandu, and there was a text which read: *I play with all my heart and soul. I become the music and the music becomes me. I feel that it is not really me playing but rather a heavenly angel, the goddess of music. Then I sometimes feel I cannot play like that again.*

"Maybe the goddess of music's in a bad mood," said the journalist, laughing.

Because it was a paper with worldwide circulation, I soon became famous all round the world. Suddenly I received an offer from an American university to teach sesandu in the department of ethnology. Oh thanks be to God! My aunt hugged me, kissed my cheek, and cried, as she was as happy as I was.

Then I started sobbing, not just because I was happy but because God had given me the opportunity to lead such a life. I felt that I had been well-named, since Immanuel means "God is with us." Yes, God has always been with you, Nuel, I said to myself.

Flying through the clouds above the Pacific Ocean, I was unable to hold back my tears. I remembered my mother selling second-hand clothes around the villages, with me following her barefoot. I recalled how I used to eat the rice cakes (*kue cucur*) and my tears flowed.

"Are you all right?" asked the girl sitting next to me.

"I'm fine. Just a bit homesick," I said.

She pushed a tissue into my hand, but I went on crying my eyes out, as all at once I recalled the little hut which my father had made when we were forced to flee the village after those forty people were murdered. He made a hut of coconut fronds. Inside there was one bamboo platform for us to sleep on. There were no chairs, just some rocks for us to sit on. When Father drowned in the Pukuafu Straits, Mother had no money. For dinner my mother and I would go down to the beach at low tide and gather shellfish and seaweed which is called *latu* in the language of Rote. There were crabs and prawns, fish and young octopus. I recalled the waves lapping at my white sand. Where the waves licked the sand, there were dozens of buried shells. When you trod on them they squirted out water, so

I would bend down, scrape away the sand, pick them up one by one, and eat them just like fried peanuts. When I had eaten my fill, mother would already have a basket full of seafood. Returning home to our hut of coconut fronds, she would cook our food, and because there was no money to buy rice, we would substitute rice by drinking the sap of the palm. It was not bad. Once I was full, I jumped up onto the sleeping platform and slept face downwards without a pillow. When I woke up in the morning, because I had too much uric acid in my body, my neck hurt when I turned to the left or the right.

Remembering that, I shook my head several times. My neck did not hurt when I turned to the window and looked at the blanket of clouds below me. Vaguely I recalled the beach where Mother and I had gathered shellfish at low tide.

"Are you going to New York?" asked the Western girl beside me.

"No. Just as far as Los Angeles," I answered.

"On business?"

"No, I'll be teaching there at the university."

"Oh, as a visiting professor," she said. After that introduction I became friends with her, when I started to get busy teaching.

One day when it was Homecoming, she invited me to her house, which was outside the city in a small town. My goodness. The house was like a palace. Her father was a physics professor. That night I slept over at her house. But as I lay in that luxurious room in that house, I recalled the hut made of coconut fronds, the sleeping platform, walking around barefoot with Mother, eating *kue cucur,* drinking the sweet palm sap.... Oh, even though I was really sleepy, I still thought about the meaning of my name. Immanuel, God is with us. Nuel, God has accompanied you even as far as America, and then I fell into a deep sleep to the rhythm of the sesandu.

Reconciliation

Pak Erman was a retired civil servant. But once he had retired he did not worry too much about his small pension. Because he had been thrifty, he had been able to buy several plots of land in Jakarta. Back then when he was still working, land in Jakarta had been cheap. Gradually he had been able to accumulate a number of plots of land and quite a few land certificates. So on the land he had bought, he built some long buildings and divided them into units. And he was the owner of these units. In each unit there lived a family or a single person. In all there were ten units and he earned rent from each one.

The walls of each unit rented out by Pak Erman were made of woven bamboo. The floors were made only of earth. Every month each tenant sprinkled the floor of their unit with water. After it was wet, it was sprinkled with sawdust and then beaten with a wisp broom. Eventually the dirt floors became fine, smooth and clean, as good as cement floors.

Even Pak Erman's house was like that. The walls were of woven bamboo and the roof of corrugated tiles. Every month his two children, Edi and Esi, watered the earthen floor, then sprinkled it with sawdust and beat it with a wisp broom until it was as smooth and even as cement.

Both the units and the house where he lived himself had walls of woven bamboo, and of course these walls had holes everywhere like a mosquito net. To block up these holes, Pak Erman and his two children made a gluey paste out of corn starch and then stuck sheets of newspaper to the walls with this paste, and once it was even they whitewashed it with lime. It was even stronger if they could stick on old cement bags. After whitewashing them, the bamboo walls looked very clean, as clean as a house of stone. In front of the house there were pots filled with flowers, so when they sat outside in the afternoon facing the *sawo* [sapodilla] and jackfruit trees, they could feel a freshness in the air.

Back then, about fifty years ago, Jakarta was not nearly as developed as now. In the gardens of both his bamboo house and the rented units, there were many different types of trees—jackfruit, papaya, *sawo*, guava, and others. And back then there were no floods like the ones we have now. After Jakarta got so developed, people planted stones everywhere, and only stones. Then they made asphalt roads without thinking about the drainage, so the roads became rivers every year in the floods.

Luckily Pak Erman's land was high enough not to be affected by the floods, and when he followed the same trend and made houses with a permanent structure, every month his unit dwellers duly paid up their rent and nobody wanted to leave because of flooding. From the one hectare of land he owned, only one area was used for monthly rental units. The rest was planted out with various crops. Although he only got his water from a well, he started a vegetable garden. And from that he also made money.

Having a vegetable garden prompted Pak Erman to rent a stall at the traditional market situated not far from his house. Initially there were all kinds of herbs and vegetables, like cabbage, ginger, different types of galangal, lemongrass, and onions. Before he had his own stall at the market, Pak Erman used to sell his produce around the housing estates. But then his stall developed. He bought a machine for grating coconuts. Then to outdo his competitors, for there were lots of people in the market who had coconut-grating machines, he took a small loan from the bank and bought a machine for pressing coconuts to make coconut milk. It became a real best-seller. Pak Erman started to get tired, but luckily his two children were able to help him. And as it happened his two children, a son and a daughter, had both already married.

So Pak Erman asked his daughter Esi's husband, Agus, who was a taxi driver, to come and help the business by running the market stall. Agus gave up his job as a taxi driver and spent every day looking after the stall with the coconut-grating and pressing machines.

But because he was basically a driver and not a trader, the market stall started losing money. He ran up debts of millions of rupiah on the coconut business. Edi and his wife, Tari, were very angry and asked Pak Erman to fire Agus. He should be told to go back to his driving. According to Edi, Agus was behaving like the director of a BUMN, a big state-owned corporation. Many of those corporations failed because their directors behaved like little kings and did not keep an eye on what their underlings were doing. For example, if the corporation bought rubber from smallholders, they bought it in bulk, but did not bother checking each bundle of rubber, so although it looked all right from the outside, the inside was rotten. And it was the same with the trucks of coconuts. Agus just told them to unload the truck without sorting through the coconuts, so when they cut them open, they found half of them were rotten, although they had already paid for all of them. That was making Pak Erman lose a lot of money.

In accordance with his son's wishes, Pak Erman dismissed Agus and Esi and, now that he had already lost his wife, handed over all of the business to Edi. He even gave his son the land certificates for the house and the rental units. Agus went back to driving taxis, but he was never able to earn enough in fares to cover the taxi rental, so the taxi company laid him off. Agus and Esi ended up with no income, could not find jobs, and were about to be evicted from their rented home. Husband and wife and their four children would just have to sleep under the flyover bridge.

Esi went berserk. She got very angry with her father, asking him why he had transferred all his certificates to Edi. She also got angry with Edi's wife, Tari. Edi defended his wife, and Esi had a big fight with Edi and Tari. Pak Erman took the middle path and asked Edi to give in, as after all Esi was his little sister. Then Esi secretly stole one of the land certificates which Pak Erman had already transferred into Edi's name. Esi felt that she was actually entitled to this certificate and pawned it to a loan shark. When Edi found out, there was another huge fight, with Edi chasing Esi with a kitchen knife as if he wanted to kill her.

Pak Erman felt that it was all his fault. He regretted transferring all his land certificates to Edi, leaving his daughter with nothing at all from his fortune. He asked Edi to forgive his sister and not watch them be evicted from the house where they were staying.

"No! She should leave the house with her husband and children. Let them just rent one of those units!" said Edi firmly.

Poor old Pak Erman was shocked. In his mind's eye, he saw the face of his wife, who had died some years ago. If his wife had still been alive, maybe there would have been a way out of this conflict, he thought.

Edi kept on complaining. "A debt of millions of rupiah on the coconuts, and it's me who has to pay off that bad debt. And that certificate has already been pawned. Thirty million's a lot of money, you know. And I have to take responsibility for all that. And then you, Father, just take their side. I swear I'm going to burn down that rental home!"

On hearing the words of his only son, he leaned heavily on his chair. His eyes clouded over. He said, "But poor Esi with her four children. One is in college and the other three are still in junior and senior high school. And Jakarta already has too many taxis. How are they going to pay for their education? They're going to be thrown out of their home because they have no money to pay the rent, and every day they're being hounded by the bank for payments. Alas, my fate now is to see my children fighting over my wealth, there's no peace between my two children…"

"But it's her who's made everything so difficult. It's me who has to pay off millions of rupiah in debts. She should be in jail. At least there's a flyover bridge for them to sleep under," said Edi.

"Oh," said their father, leaning even more heavily on his chair. His vision became worse and worse.

It was like receiving an electric shock when he saw the two of them quarrelling violently. Esi was throttling her elder brother, then he punched his sister in the mouth. Pak Erman could only shout, "It's like all your feelings of love for one another as brother and sister have disappeared. It's a civil war, a civil war between brother and sister!" he shouted.

Edi's wife, Tari, who had just kept out of it until that point, also started to get involved. Especially when she saw her sister-in-law scratching her husband with her long nails and his cheeks bleeding. Tari could not hold back any longer and, raising her voice, she said, "After deceiving us and stealing from us, now you're behaving like thugs!"

"What? But look at how your husband has punched me and broken my tooth! I'm going to report him to the police. He'll go to prison for five years!" shrieked Esi.

"But you'll also get five years for scratching my husband's face. Five years!"

Esi sprang up and grabbed Tari's hair, and the two of them pulled each other's hair and scratched each other, and then started pushing each other hard. Pak Erman broke up the fight. "That's enough! Don't make me lose my temper. You both know I'm a former *pencak silat* [martial arts] champion, don't you!"

Then he took them to the hospital to have their wounds treated.

The civil war abated. Edi, Esi, and Tari just sat quietly in the car as it took them to the hospital.

"Hm…I still have a certificate for two thousand square meters of land which has not been transferred to Edi's name. I'll give that land to Esi. But in the meantime I'm going to mortgage it and give Esi the money as start-up capital for a business," said Pak Erman abruptly. Edi looked put out.

"Can you open a food stall selling beef-rib soup?" Pak Erman asked his daughter.

"Of course she can't," interjected Edi. "How can the wife of a taxi driver start a food stall selling rib soup!"

"Now what?" bellowed Esi.

"If you two don't stop fighting I'm going to drive into an electricity pylon!" said Pak Erman.

They kept quiet.

"First I have to have some false teeth fitted, then I'll open the beef-rib soup stall," retorted Esi.

"No problem," said Pak Erman.

Once at the hospital they found that Esi's tooth had not come out, she just had a swollen lip. And a nurse just smeared the scratches on Edi's face with a red ointment. On the way home the two siblings just kept quiet and so did their sister-in-law, Tari.

"Now pay attention, I don't want you two fighting anymore. Everything's fair now. My wealth has now been divided up evenly. You, Edi, have got some of it and, Esi, you have got some too."

"And what about that certificate which this frizzy-headed imbecile has pawned?" said Edi gesturing towards Esi, whose curly hair, since she had given birth, had turned almost kinky.

"We'll get that back. Just don't worry about it!"

All the way home they didn't say anything. Pak Erman knew what was in the hearts of his son and daughter-in-law. As a former *pencak silat* champion, he would take action if they started fighting again.

When they got home, Pak Erman asked them all to sit around the dining table. Then he led them in prayer, asking the Lord for forgiveness for the behavior of his children and beseeching that there might be peace and love between them always. Before they had finished praying there was suddenly an earthquake. They were startled. Pak Erman just carried on praying.

When the long prayers were finally over, Esi immediately blurted out. "What a pity it was only a small earth tremor. If it had been a proper disaster, we would have got help like food, drink, clothes, blankets, money, and tents from all round the world. My family and I would not be evicted by the owner of our rental unit."

The December Floods

The December rains flooded the narrow streets of the city. Despite this I needed to go out and visit my friend's mother, who lived in a very narrow street in the middle of the city. Because her house was not far from a small river, it was inevitable that it would be affected by the December floods. But the floods were not too serious. The water level only came up to my calves. Perhaps because her house was near the river the water could drain off quickly. I rolled up my trouser legs as far as my knees and walked carrying my shoes. When I got to the front porch of the house I put my shoes back on and rolled my trousers down again before knocking on the door.

My friend's mother led me to the living room and said, "Oh, child, it's so good you still think of me, and you've come to see me even though it's raining," hugging and kissing me affectionately. I felt happy. It was as if she were my own mother. We sat facing one another in the living room. It was not long before my hostess said, "When it's cold we need to drink something hot, right?" Then getting up she asked, "Coffee or tea?"

"Coffee please, Ma," I answered.

After we'd had a drink together and a piece of cake, we continued chatting.

"I am really sorry that when Roni died, I was overseas doing my doctorate."

As I said those words, I looked into her eyes. Her face was melancholy, her eyes were tearful. I went on, "The strange thing was that a little before he died we spoke on the phone. I urged him to keep his spirits up in his last days."

"Thank you, child. Although you never became his brother-in-law, I'm happy that you never stopped being friends with Roni. If Roni ever did wrong by you, please forgive him. Of course you know that Roni made a lot of mistakes in his business dealings—a business that was supposed to support his widowed mother and his fatherless younger brothers and sisters."

"I understand, Ma, and I'm proud of the tenacity that Roni showed in all his business dealings. He was very enterprising when it came to earning money to support his mother and his younger brothers and sisters. He was my mentor, he showed me how to earn money by doing business without any capital. Thanks to him I learned how to make money and was able to fund my own schooling through high school and university, and even go on to study for my doctorate overseas, and now I've been able to become a university lecturer. But because my salary as a lecturer is fairly small, I have set up a small business on the side and do pretty well out of it. I still remember when I was in high school, staying in a hostel. When my father died, my life looked bleak. Roni turned up to be my mentor. He told me, 'Don't be sad, making money is easy'.

"'What do you mean, easy?" I asked.

"'Knock on the doors of your friends in the hostel and ask if there's anyone who needs their washing done.'

"So I did other people's washing. And I earned money to pay for the hostel and to pay my school fees and to buy books. But it wasn't just that. One day Roni took me to the *dokar* [horse-drawn buggy] terminal at the edge of the city. I was amazed to see how he interacted so easily with the *dokar* drivers. It looked so effortless how he joked and bantered with them. Every day we had to provide them with several sacks of fresh grass, so in effect we became their fresh grass suppliers. But Roni did not do the hard work himself. He was a real businessman, paying other people to cut the grass and put it in the sacks. We became white-collar grass gatherers, in smart suits and ties. Cool, right, Ma?"

Roni's mother smiled. Her expression showed pride in her beloved son but also how much she missed him.

"But it didn't stop there, Ma. One day Roni turned up at the hostel and took me on a walk to the traditional market. He observed the high prices being asked for betel leaves and chillis. That very same day he took me out of town to look for betel leaves and chillis. 'Amazing,' I said. In short, it was Roni who taught me all about economics so that I was able to earn enough money to put myself through school, up to becoming a doctor of economics, Ma."

"Thank goodness for that. But what a pity you never became Roni's brother-in-law," said the woman.

"Oh, that doesn't matter a bit. You're still like my real mother. You don't need to worry about your old age. You have a son in me," I said, pointing at my own heart.

Roni's mother began to weep. And outside the rain got heavier and heavier. The sound of the rain thundering down on the roof and the wind howling was deafening. The level of the flood water in the narrow street had risen. Luckily the level of the house had been raised, but I still complained, "Now I won't be able to get home, Ma."

"Just sleep here. It's not a big house but there's a sofa," she said.

So we passed the rest of the afternoon talking and talking until nightfall.

"How's your wife, how're your children? Well, I hope?"

I sighed deeply when she asked about my family. But I forced myself to speak honestly. "Oh, Ma, I'm sorry, I must tell you how things turned out for me in my marriage. Once my wife came out of the mental hospital, it was me who looked after her. One day when I had just finished bathing her and changing her clothes, a guest arrived unexpectedly. I was busy welcoming the guest and forgot to put our telephone number in my wife's shirt. I was chatting away happily to my guest without realizing that my wife had gone round to the back of the house, where we had built a three-meter-high wall. She climbed over the wall and ran away, and has been missing ever since."

"Goodness me! Life has been tough on you, child. You've looked everywhere for her, have you? Oh my, you poor thing..."

"Yes, I've looked for her everywhere but haven't been able to find her," I said.

"And what about children?"

"I just have one daughter and she has just finished her studies to become a doctor," I said.

"I've lost the backbone of my family and you've lost your rib bone, your companion. Fortunately your daughter succeeded in becoming a doctor. Thanks be to God," said the woman.

Suddenly Margarita, Roni's younger sister, appeared. She was once my girlfriend. It felt as if the house had been struck by lightning.

"Dinner's ready. Please come into the dining room," said Margarita before disappearing out the back.

"So Gita's here, Ma?" I asked.

"Yes."

"With her husband?"

"With her only child."

"Where's her husband?"

"That's a long story. I'll tell you all about it after dinner," said the woman cutting off my curiosity.

"It's only a simple dinner, I'm sorry if it's not very tasty," said Margarita.

"It's amazing, just like food in a restaurant," I said praising her.

"After her husband passed away, Gita became a single parent and earned a living for her child. We could make a decent living with that business. Roni left us nothing. Ida, Gita's younger sister, had already got married to an American, but her husband is very stingy. Ida has to work her socks off. But the main thing is she can manage in this time of crisis," said the woman. "Only, what I worry about is restaurants. With so much food around I fear that disease, diabetes, will get them like what happened to Roni and Gita's late husband, Rudi. They were both good at finding money to put food on the table but hopeless about what they actually ate. And that's why they got diabetes. But you, young Herman, look fresh and well. You don't look sick," said the woman. "What's your blood sugar reading?"

"It's normal, Ma. But there's an illness that's even more serious than diabetes or high cholesterol," I said.

"What illness is that?" asked Gita.

"Loneliness. Losing Adam's rib."

"Oh, come, on, I thought you were really sick. A man like you can easily find another rib. In fact here she is!" said the woman nodding towards Margarita.

Gita bowed her head.

"If you want to come back to me, Gita…. Aren't you a pharmacy graduate? I'll open a drug store. I'm also keen to have a garden so that my yard at home becomes a living apothecary. My business on the side has always been farming. I have a coconut plantation with a hundred coconut palms with pure oil that can be used for medicinal purposes. I am grateful to Almighty God because I actually came from very poor beginnings. When I was small, most days I was only given boiled corn to eat. When I went to school, my lunch pack was fried dried corn which was as hard as stones and my teeth had to be strong as pincers to chew it, and it made a sharp crunchy noise. When I came home from school, I turned into a monkey who climbed all kinds of trees—mango, *duet* [wild cherry], mulberry, tamarillo which grew on a very tall straight tree, and *jeruk Bali* [big grapefruits] with their ripe red flesh. All disappeared into my stomach. Once I was full, I didn't go straight home but stayed out playing football until dusk. My mother snapped that if I went on like that I would turn into a monkey!

"So that was my childhood growing up as a poor boy. Maybe that's why I haven't got diabetes or high cholesterol or anything like that. Praise be to God that I was poor but always healthy. What a shame that a poor child like me lost his mentor who taught him how to make money. The difference between us was that Roni accumulated fat on his body while I accumulated knowledge in my brain. But whatever happens to me in my life, I will never forget Roni. And because of this, all the good things that Roni did for me in my life, I have come back to this house. Because of this I suddenly remembered Roni's mother and younger sisters, so my feet carried me to this house and unexpectedly I have rediscovered my Adam's rib which I lost years ago. You're right tonight, Ma. Gita, your mother agrees that I've returned to you," I said to Margarita.

Gita said nothing. Suddenly she rubbed tears from her cheeks. Perhaps she was happy about what I had said to her.

Gita's mother took a deep breath and then began to tell her story. "As you say, Roni was good at making money, but he got fat and was struck down by diabetes. As for his little sister, she never suffered from this illness. Roni inherited this problem from his father's side of the family, whereas Gita inherited her mother's stamina. My stamina. What I can't stop thinking about is the way Roni dealt with his hour of death, behaving as if he was a very important person. A little while before he died, he asked to be moved to a first-class room. It was the best room in the hospital, and he asked the nurse to pick flowers and put them all around his bed. The temperature in his room was as cold as the North Pole. Maybe Roni felt that as he had worked so hard all his life to make money, he was going to die like a king," said the woman recalling her son's last days.

"Mom, you shouldn't talk like that," said Margarita.

Even after we had finished dinner, the rain had still not stopped and went on thundering down on the roof. If there had been a waterwheel, there was certainly enough water falling to generate electricity.

Gita brought a pillow and a blanket and put them on the sofa in the living room. I stretched out on the sofa—and then suddenly there was a power cut. In the darkness, all sorts of fuzzy memories came back to me. Roni was really very good at making money, but as the saying went, however clever the little squirrel was at leaping from branch to branch, sometimes he would fall. Roni once startled me when he fell. This is what happened. One Sunday Roni turned up in my room. "Herman," he said, "Have you paid your school fees and hostel boarding fees yet?"

"No, not yet," I said.

Roni told me to go with him to a garment factory which produced shirts. "Take these boxes of shirts to this address, OK?" he said, loading the boxes onto a *becak*.

"Aren't you coming along?" I asked.

"No, I'm staying here as the guarantor. You don't understand how it works. This is trading without any capital. Later, when they've paid for the shirts you're taking to them, bring the money back here. We pay the Chinese boss and then divide the profit between the two of us," he said.

"Oh, so that's how it works," I said and went off to the address he had given me.

After I'd brought the money back, we went to a restaurant to have lunch. As we were enjoying the benefit of our efforts in trading without capital, suddenly two big men came up to us. They looked like debt collectors.

"When are you going to pay your debts?" said one of them.

"Sorry, my mother's just had to have an operation, so I can't pay it back yet," said Roni.

"But you've done nothing but make promises for the last five years," he said, then took the plates and glasses off the table and smashed them to bits. Roni was hit by broken glass and got a cut on his forehead.

"Next month, if you can't pay your debts, the amount will go up!" said one of the two debt collectors, and then they left.

I took Roni to the doctor's. After being treated, Roni wanted to divide up the money, but I refused, saying, "Keep that money to help pay off your debts." And then I left and walked back to the hostel.

That was the first time I had knowingly seen Roni in trouble.

The second time was at the time of the G30SPKI incident, when Roni decided he wanted to sell medicines to this group of people. And in fact the sales were fantastic. It looked like Roni was going to be rich, but then unfortunately he was arrested and taken to prison where he was beaten up badly. When he came out of prison, he looked for me. I was shocked to see his face all black and blue.

After the memories came dreams. I dreamt that I was a *romusha* forced laborer who was being carried off to some place. In the middle of the ocean we were all crowded together to sleep along with a lot of dried coconuts. Suddenly I filled a sack with coconuts and tied it up tightly, then jumped down into the ocean and swam holding onto the coconuts in the sack. Eventually we were cast ashore on an island full of guava trees growing everywhere. Because

I was hungry I ate the fruit until I was full. Then suddenly a wild boar with big tusks came out of the forest to chase me. I jumped up a coconut palm, but in my haste I fell!

Plop! I'd actually fallen off the sofa.

A moment later Gita was beside me carrying a candle. "What's the matter, brother?" she asked.

"There's nothing the matter, I just fell off the sofa because I was dreaming that I was being chased by a wild boar after swimming a long way," I said, rubbing my face which was wet from drops of water falling through a leak in the roof.

Original Titles

The original Indonesian titles of the short stories in this collection are shown in the table below. The English translations are based on the stories as they appeared in *Matias Akankari* (Jakarta, Kosa Kata Kita, 2015). While the stories were written over a period of decades, neither the author nor his heirs were able to provide Lontar with complete data regarding their original publication dates or sources. For this lack of information, the publisher apologizes.

No.	English Title	Original Title
01.	The Anatomy of Travel	Anatomi Perjalanan
02.	The Water Buffalo Sellers	Penjual Kerbau
03.	An Impoverished Village Far Away from Anywhere	Dusun yang Sangat Melarat
04.	Karawang – Bekasi	Karawang–Bekasi
05.	Between Beirut and Bali	Antara Beirut dan Bali
06.	Woven Cloth	Kain Tenun
07.	When the Jackfruit Tree Was Bearing Fruit	Ketika Nangka Sedang Berbuah
08.	Sandalwood Fans	Kipas Cendana
09.	The Thatched House with a Stone Wall	Rumah Ilalang Berpagar Batu
10.	Pond of Gold	Kolam Emas
11.	An Aria to Travel	Nyanyian Perjalanan
12.	The Pearl Family	Keluarga Mutiara
13.	A Family of Wanderers	Keluarga Perantau
14.	Sculpture	Patung
15.	The Absent-Minded Lawyer	Pengacara Pikun

No.	English Title	Original Title
16.	When I Became a Papuan	Ketika Aku Menjadi Orang Papua
17.	Sesandu	Sesandu
18.	Reconciliation	Perdamaian
19.	December Floods	Banjir Bulan Desember

Biographical Information

GERSON POYK was born on 16 June 1931 in Namodale, East Nusa Tenggara, and died at the age of 86 on 24 February 2017 in Depok, West Java. First a teacher, then a journalist, Poyk was a prolific writer. He wrote novels and short stories but also poetry and plays. After publishing his first book in 1964, by the end of his life in 2017, Poyk had published thirty titles, including thirteen novels, fourteen collections of short stories, one collection of poetry, a book of journalistic writing, and one book of philosophical reflections. The recipient of numerous literary and non-literary awards—including the Adinegoro award for journalism, the SEA-Write Award, the Life Time Achievement Award from Kompas, and the Indonesian Cultural Award (Anugerah Kebudayaan), the government's highest prize in the field of culture—Poyk is often referred to as the story teller of Eastern Indonesia.

GILL WESTAWAY has lived in Indonesia on and off since 1993 and currently resides on Lombok, running a small guesthouse near Senggigi. In her former incarnation working for the British Council, she collaborated closely with writers and artists in Kenya, Indonesia, the Philippines, and Sri Lanka, managing and chairing literary events to promote literature in English and other languages. Having specialized in Translation Studies at Exeter University in the UK, she now works as a freelance translator and editor and is keen to help gain wider exposure for Indonesian literature around the world.